# The Wysman

## Dorothy A. Winsor

Inspired
Quill

Published by Inspired Quill: May 2020

First Edition

Chief Editor: Sara-Jayne Slack
Cover Design: Marco Pennacchietti
Cover Text: Venetia Jackson
Typeset in Minion Pro

Paperback ISBN: 978-1-908600-95-0
eBook ISBN: 978-1-908600-96-7
Print Edition

Printed in the United Kingdom
1 2 3 4 5 6 7 8 9 10

**Inspired Quill Publishing, UK**
**Business Reg. No. 7592847**
www.inspired-quill.com

# Praise for Dorothy Winsor

*Dorothy Winsor's novel presents an intriguing and well-drawn world, with a very likeable lead. An exciting, adventurous, and thoughtful YA fantasy novel.*

– Dr. Una McCormack,
*New York Times Bestselling Author*

*Dorothy A. Winsor is a meticulous writer who expertly balances intelligence and delight.*

– Saladin Ahmed,
*Hugo, Nebula, and Gemmell Awards finalist*

*Journeys: A Ghost Story, is a very good tale that, without any real surprises, still manages to surprise. There's a well-wrought aura of melancholy that permeates the story, even in the funny moments. Another author I'll keep an eye out for in the future.*

– Fletcher Vredenburgh,
*Black Gate Magazine*

*[In Finders Keepers], the action is brisk, emotions are deep, and the moral message is subtle but strong, providing excellent depth for all readers, young and not so young. Great story – I loved it as an adult and think it is a wonderful book for older kids and young adults. Five Stars.*

– Melinda Hills,
*Readers' Favorite*

For Dan

*Wysmen and Wyswomen arise in every generation. The faithful know them by their courage and wisdom, and by their selfless care for the weak and the needy.*

*– The Book of the Wys*

# Chapter 1

A S SOON AS I stepped out into the empty castle courtyard, I felt it. The wind puffed through my clothes and walked a chill finger down my back. It wanted me, and it wanted me now. It had things to tell me, then. My heart sped up. I hitched across the courtyard, amid signs of the castle household just beginning to stir. Smoke rose from the kitchen chimney. A boy was just vanishing into the stables carrying a bucket of whatever horses need in the morning. Other than the boy, the wind and I were the only ones around.

I hobbled through the gate from the main courtyard into the keep around the old tower. Damp shadows pooled inside the keep's mossy walls. In the dawn quiet, my crutch thudded even more loudly than usual as I crossed the flagstones toward the stairs leading to the top of the castle wall.

"Stop right there, boy."

I jumped, then caged my teeth around a curse. Absorbed in the feel of the wind, I hadn't even noticed the baby-faced guard looking down at me from the walkway. If I'd been that dozy when I lived on the streets, I'd be shivering in just my skin while some thief sold my clothes—fleas and all—on the other side of town.

"Stop? Why?"

"You're not allowed up here." The guard rested his hand on the hilt of his sword. I'd not seen him before, so he was new and nervous as a fresh gang recruit guarding his territory. His accent said he was from somewhere deep in the farm country of Longrass.

I hesitated. The castle was still new territory for me, too. How hard could I push? "Horse spit. Prince Beran himself picked me to be his Wysman someday because I can read the wind. I do it up there every morning."

"When I'm on duty, you don't." A smudge of struggling moustache quivered on the guard's upper lip. "As a matter of fact, I'm banning you from the keep while I'm guarding it. That stuff you fool with is dangerous." He shuddered. "Sorcery."

"Don't call it that. The divine Powers move in all the elements. When I read the wind, I just channel their energy. All our ancestors used to do it."

"I don't care. We're civilized now."

A gust of wind slapped my hair against my cheeks. *Hurry*, it demanded.

"I'm coming up," I said. "Move away if you don't like

it." One eye on the guard, I set my good foot on the first step and dragged the crooked foot and my crutch after me. The guard watched for a wild-eyed moment, before backing away to give me room. My shoulders eased. The guard and his sword should just stay over there where the wall turned.

I heaved myself up the last step and looked over the parapet. The fields on the other side of the river still lay quiet in the new day. A yellow-green haze of shoots blanketed the recently planted earth. Once again, the world was reborn. There'd be much worth celebrating at the feast of Darklight four days from now, assuming you had the coin. But then, most days were worth celebrating if you had the coin.

The wind flung grit into my face. *I'm coming,* I thought. *Keep your trousers on.* When I reached the place where the crenellations were wider apart, I slid the leather bag off my shoulder onto the flat stone between them, undid the flap, and pulled out the bundle of carved wooden pieces. One tug on the leather thong, and the pieces snapped erect to become my wind-reading box. I brushed my fingers reverently over one rune-carved side, still awed by the box's beauty, even now, half a year after Prince Beran had given it to me. The runes dated from the long-ago time of the Wys Ones. Since then, Rinlanders had acquired learning and a holy Faith, or as the baby-faced guard would put it, the country had become "civilized." Underlying it all, though, the wild force of elemental energy still lingered. I'd felt it in the streets of Rin City, and here in the castle, it was so strong it shocked me that most folks didn't even notice it was there. Beneath my fingertips, the box throbbed with it, making its earthy taste pool in my mouth. My heart pulsed in my throat.

From my bag, I pulled the velvet pouch and dumped a heap of bright confetti into my palm. I closed my eyes and stilled my thoughts. *Hush...Let go...Make space for the Powers...Let go.*

Like water pouring into an empty pitcher, an energy that wasn't mine flooded me from hair to heel. My eyes snapped open. I glimpsed the guard edging closer, but I fenced out all thoughts of anything else, stared into the wind box, and chose the invocation.

"The Powers move in the wind," I murmured. "Wind sweeps between Earth and Sky. It whispers of where it's been and where it's going. I humbly beg you, Mother Earth, Father Sky. Use the white of the North Wind—"

I flung some of the paper bits into the box, and a faint wisp of pine woods tickled my nose.

"—the blue of the East Wind—"

I threw a second pinch of paper. In my mind's eye, a pheasant soared from a field into endless sky.

"—the red of the South Wind—"

More paper bits. Heat and the smell of salt water brushed across my face.

"—the green of the West Wind."

I tossed the last of the colored paper. The trees of a

great forest rustled in my ears.

"Tell me what lies ahead, behind, and beyond for your child, Jarka."

A finger of wind slid through the holes in the runes and swirled the paper in the wind box. I puffed out my cheeks and blew, mixing my breath with the wind, tuning it to my life and the things that mattered to me.

The wind-blown world jumped to life so strongly my head spun. All things that had ever been or would be left their marks, and I felt as if the wind was trying to blow them all into my brain at once. It spun itself into a tight whirl, and blew a sharp, flowery scent up my nose just before my head exploded in pain. Stark terror froze my heart, then vanished into a cold dark. I twisted away and from the outside now, I saw a tall figure fling a shorter one to the ground.

With a wordless cry, I jerked all the way free of the vision.

"What have you called up?" The guard tripped closer, his eyes wide enough to show white at all the edges, his round cheeks drained of color. "Stop it!"

Struggling for enough air to speak, I shook my head. Finally, I managed to choke out, "Believe me, if I could, I would."

I peered into the wind box, swearing under my breath. The only thing I saw now was fluttering paper. I wouldn't be able to read for myself again until the wind had something new to show me. I stood over the box, breathing hard. Someone had hurt or would hurt a smaller person. My mind raced. This was my reading, so the vision must be connected to me somehow. Who would I care about? My thoughts flew like an arrow to Cousin Lyssa and her daughter Izzy. Could Lyssa's new husband, Clovyan, have hurt one of them or be about to? As far as I knew, Clovyan had never hit Izzy, but he slapped Lyssa around and had once beaten me savagely enough to make me head out the door. Not that I cared. Life on the streets had been better. Come to think of it, could that beating be what I saw? The Powers knew I relived it often enough in my nightmares, and the wind mixed up past, present, and future, like a cook stirring stew.

A familiar flush of shame washed through me at the memory. I'd been fifteen when Clovyan beat me bloody. I should have been able to fight him off, should have been able to keep him from hitting my cousin, too. I lifted the tip of my crutch and thumped it down again.

From the main courtyard came the sounds of running boots and the stable master shouting for a groom. Perched on the wall, I could see the city sloping down the hill outside the castle gates in a rolling sea of golden thatched roofs. The streets were beginning to stir too. I should check on Lyssa. If Clovyan had hit her again, maybe I could finally convince her to leave him. Not right away though. Clovyan would take an hour or so to open the tailor shop and then be off to the Broken Cart for his morning mug of ale. If I waited, the coast would be clear. I realized I'd crushed the velvet bag in my hand. That cold blank near the vision's end made me nervous. I'd never felt it before, and it was too much like...well, like how I imagined death would feel.

I scraped up the paper bits, collapsed the box, stuffed it into my bag, and worked my way slowly down the steps. From the corner of my eye, I could see the guard making shooing motions to hurry me along. When I passed through the gate to the main courtyard, I found stable hands, kitchen workers, and guards all streaming toward the Great Hall for morning prayers. I sped up, meaning to stow my bag in my room and hustle to the Hall. Serving at morning prayers was one of my apprentice duties. If I was late, everyone would know, and at morning prayers, "everyone" included the king. All I needed was for him to decide I was useless and kick me out the way Clovyan had.

I shook my head. I wished Clovyan out of it almost as much as I wished Lyssa out of his house. Stone me if I didn't make sure both wishes came true the first day Beran named me his Wysman and I could borrow his power to turn the Tower Guards loose on people like Clovyan.

# Chapter 2

WITH A JINGLE of brass rings, I shoved past the leather curtain forming what was, in my opinion, an inadequately secure door to my room in the boys' dormitory. Unfortunately, I found Dugan's sour face just emerging from a red velvet tunic he was pulling over his head. The gold shirt he wore as one of King Thien's squires lay in a heap on the floor. He must have been freed from his day's duties again because his family was in town. I set my crutch down carefully in the litter of his dropped clothes. Dugan seemed to believe it was outrageous to expect him to carry his dirty clothes to the laundry basket at the end of the hall. More than once I'd seen him sniff several shirts before picking out one to wear. Much more dignified.

"I thought I smelled street trash." With far too much admiration for his own muscles, Dugan smoothed the tunic over his chest. "Did Adrya dismiss you yet?" He shook his head sadly. "She could have chosen so much better."

By "better," Dugan meant himself, which would have been sad if it weren't hilarious. I played deaf and dropped my carry bag into my clothes chest.

"Hey, street boy. I'm talking to you. It's disrespectful to turn your back on your betters."

I groped among my few clothes for the oiled paper packet of horehound drops I'd bought as a Darklight gift for Izzy. I might as well take the sweets with me since I didn't know when I'd have another chance. I lifted the frayed winter cloak the dormitory master had scrounged for me, too warm for this fine morning. Where was the cursed candy?

"Is this what you're looking for?" Dugan asked.

I pivoted. Dugan stood three paces away, tossing the packet of candy up and catching it again. My hand tightened on my crutch. "You had no right to go through my things. Give it to me." I grabbed for the packet, leaned too far, and had to hop to regain my balance.

Dugan backed up, tossed the packet, and yanked his hand away so it thudded to the floor, where he knew I'd have an awkward struggle to reach it. "I was just checking your pathetic little pile of 'things' for fleas." Dugan nudged the packet with his toe. "You don't belong here, and you know it. Adrya was a fool to make you her apprentice instead of me. She promised my father she would."

I'd heard about this so-called promise before. As far as

I could tell, Dugan or his father had made it up. "At least I can read the Wys Ones' runes." I pointed to a row of runes carved on the wall, optimistically admonishing a room used by teen aged boys to seek the true way. "What does that say again?"

Dugan's ears grew red. "You're probably stealing the gold chain right off Adrya's neck, but she's too blind to notice." He lifted his booted foot and stomped on the packet of candy.

I lunged. Dugan scrambled backward quickly enough that my fingers only brushed over his tunic and I toppled to the floor. His hoot of laughter cut off when I swung my crutch and clouted him on the ankle. He howled and hopped but stayed upright and scuttled from the room.

I lay for a moment among Dugan's dirty clothes, wishing I'd managed to cram the tip of my crutch into his gut. As usual, my wish might as well have been spent on sprouting wings and flying. The packet of candy lay just beyond my right fingers. I hooked it closer. When I pinched the packet, what had been hard drops shifted like dust. It didn't matter, I told myself. Izzy would be happy to lick it off her grubby palm. I struggled to my knees and then my feet, stuffed the packet in my pocket, and headed out of the dormitory on my way to the Hall. The dormitory beat the streets by a long stone's throw, but there were moments when I ached for my old bed in Lyssa's house—the way it had been before she married Clovyan.

Picking my way through the castle hallways always felt like picking my way through a maze, partly because I was still figuring out what territory I could safely enter, but mostly because the architect must have been drunk. I hurried along a passage that zigged left before zagging right and emptying into the king's small waiting room behind the Great Hall. He wasn't there yet, thank the Powers, but Adrya was, dressed in her white overtunic and carrying the ancient copy of *The Book of the Wys*. She was pacing in front of the tapestry that showed a vixen with her sharp nose and reddish-brown hair. I occasionally considered pointing out the resemblance but had never gathered the nerve. Her rose perfume drifted after her.

She halted mid-step. "Where have you been?"

"Dropping my wind box in my room. I have to go see my cousin as soon as prayers are over." No point in mentioning the quarrel with Dugan. I didn't want to find out if she'd take my side.

"What about your lessons?" Adrya asked. "Can't you wait a day until the holiday starts?"

I pictured the safe, quiet library, smelling of books and scrolls, and shook off a pang of longing. "I'm sorry, but the wind showed me someone being beaten. I want to try one more time to get her to see sense."

She tapped her toe, and I knew what she was about to say—again. "She told the Tower Guard I sent to stay out of her business."

"I know she can be a fool, but maybe this time will be

different."

"Jarka, when a woman is a fool about a man, she's not going to listen to a sixteen-year-old boy. Believe me. I've been a fool myself."

I tried and failed to picture Adrya mooning over a man. To me, she always seemed as tightly tied down as her hair.

"Do you want to become a Wysman or not?" Adrya went on. "You're here to learn so you can advise your king on how best to govern, not look after your cousin."

I nodded at the book Adrya carried. "That says Wysones also serve the poor and needy. Isn't that right?"

Adrya's mouth pressed into a thin line. "Your cousin is not poor." She held up a hand to stop me speaking. "You need to be here. A Wysone serves everybody by advising a king. I'm thinking of your own good too. If you neglect your studies, Prince Beran might decide you won't be useful enough to keep on."

That thought was *not* getting a toehold in my head. I didn't have time for this anyway. Once Clovyan finished his ale, he'd head home. "It's late, isn't it?" I hobbled toward the door to the Great Hall. "Shouldn't I be getting things ready?"

Adrya waved me toward the Hall. "Go."

The eyes of the crowd in the Hall all swung my way as I entered, slamming me back for a moment. Usually morning prayers were attended only by the castle household and their families. But six months ago, Thien had survived an assassination attempt by the Lord of the Uplands, and folks were still twitchy. It turned out the king was too, because Thien had decided to use the Darklight Festival as an occasion to require all the nobility, large and small, to retake their loyalty oaths to the crown. They must have already arrived in bigger numbers than I'd realized. The only windows in the Hall were high up near the ceiling, which always made me itch because of the way that blocked out the wind. This morning it also left the Hall over warm and thick with the smell of sweat.

Conversations which had halted when I entered rose again when folks saw I wasn't the king. I hauled myself up the single step to the platform and opened the cupboard built into the carved wooden stand. I lit the silver brazier with a sulfur stick, inhaling the pleasantly biting scent, then filled a tiny cup with incense and set it next to the brazier. I withdrew to the rear of the platform and pressed my back against the wall, waiting for Adrya and the king and thinking about Lyssa. She really was a fool, and I could feel my worry giving way to irritation. She was choosing to stay with Clovyan, but Izzy was helpless to leave on her own. I didn't understand how Lyssa could risk Clovyan hitting her kid. She'd seen what he did to me and I was sure she was horrified. *Not enough to leave Clovyan and go with you*, sneered a voice in my head. Which was true enough. But she must have known I could take care of myself whereas Izzy was only five.

Folks on one side of the room stiffened, which was all

the warning I needed before King Thien strode in. The king was tall and dark with the manner of a man used to having people jump when he turned a hawk-sharp look their way. He appeared to ignore the people in the Hall, but I'd learned from experience that Thien would notice anything out of the ordinary and expect an explanation of it from the adviser who should know.

The crowd dipped into bows and curtsies, their heads lowering in a rainbow wave of colorful wool and satin that flowed from the front of the room to the back. Overhead, the banners of Rinland's eight provinces stirred sluggishly. The king moved to his usual place at the front of the crowd and turned to face Adrya, who'd followed him in and was setting *The Book of the Wys* on the stand. The visitors held themselves so erect they almost quivered and turned slightly toward the king, watching him while pretending not to.

I smothered a sneer. The so-called "quality" would let Thien kick their rear ends if they thought the kick would boost them higher than their neighbors. My gaze caught on a sparrow hopping along a rafter. The sparrow flicked its tail, and someone in the crowd swore. I suppressed a smile. Some misfortunes fell on rich and poor alike.

Adrya closed her eyes and stood with one hand clutching the Wyswoman's pendant hanging around her neck. Gradually, silence spread through the room, as people settled down to hear what Adrya would find in today's reading. I had to admit she read truth in *The Book* as if the Powers were whispering it in her ear. Just the week before, she'd read a passage about how wrong it was to take more than your due, and the next day, the Steward dismissed an assistant for stealing. According to the Faith, anyone could find truth in *The Book*. You opened it, and the first passage your eyes fell on told you how to act rightly that day. I'd done it myself. Good advice was good advice.

The silence stretched. Someone coughed. A woman put a hand on her little girl's shoulder to hold her still. A young guard yawned so widely I had to lock my jaw to keep from mirroring him. I silently urged Adrya to get on with things. Clovyan wouldn't stay at the ale house forever, and the thought of running into him made my armpits ooze.

Adrya flung three pinches of incense into the brazier and waited while threads of fragrant smoke drifted into the faces of the people in front. She opened *The Book* and read in a clear voice: "'We live as part of a great giving and taking. Water bubbles from beneath Mother Earth and flows through the land. It empties into the sea where Father Sky dips down to meet it and draw it to himself, only to send it to us again as rain for our fields. So our divine parents care for us as we care for our own children. To harm them for our own desires would be an abomination.'"

In the stillness after Adrya stopped reading, my feet felt stuck to the floor. The reading from *The Book* matched my fears about Izzy too closely for comfort. I glanced at Adrya. She should interpret the reading now, and I wanted to reach into her mouth and drag the words out quickly. Instead, she was dawdling, her eyes on a man front and center in the crowd. He had to be a visitor because I didn't know him even by sight. He stood next to Dugan, and he also shared Dugan's broad-shouldered build. They looked enough alike to be related, but as far as Dugan had said, his parents were the only family who'd come to town to re-say their fealty oath, and the man next to Dugan looked only a few years older than my roommate. The woman on Dugan's other side was undoubtedly his mother. She kept straightening his collar or fussing with his hair while he twitched irritably. I looked back at the man next to Dugan. Under Adrya's scrutiny, he'd frozen like a pickpocket with a watchman's hand on his shoulder. What was that about?

Adrya released the man from her gaze and turned to the crowd. "Among the blessings the Powers send, children are the most precious. We owe them our care as others cared for us when we were young. The wheel of life turns, and we all change places. This is a blessing, not a loss."

The man next to Dugan snapped his gaze straight ahead, his face going as white as his shirt. What Adrya said seemed tame enough to me, but it hit him like a punch in the head. In contrast, Dugan's mother had gone red. Dugan's eyes shifted from one to the other. He looked confused, but then he often looked that way. Adrya's shot at the man had to be deliberate. I didn't know what she was after, but this wouldn't be the first time I'd seen her bend her interpretation in ways she thought would be useful to Thien.

"*The Book of the Wys* reminds us of how strong we are when we care for one another," Adrya went on. "So how fitting it is that you are gathered to pledge your loyalty on the Festival of Darklight, one of the two days of the year when light and dark share the world equally, in perfect balance. May the Powers bless us all." She closed *The Book*.

At last. The crowd in the Hall waited while Thien left the way he'd come, with Adrya at his heels. I damped the brazier and hitched rapidly after them. I looked back once to see Adrya's target shouldering his way toward the big double doors at the Hall's other end, having apparently abandoned Dugan and his mother to wade through the crowd on their own.

Usually Thien passed straight through the waiting room. Today though, I found him still there facing Adrya. I edged toward the door, ready to go as soon as the king released us.

"What was all that about Rosin?" Thien asked. "Were you talking about that old business with his uncle?"

I recognized the name from hearing Dugan boast endlessly about "my father, Lord Rosin Stonebridge." So despite the man's youth, he *was* Dugan's father. He had to have been younger than I was now when Dugan was born.

That was what I called starting early.

"I didn't think it would hurt to remind him of the rules." Adrya gripped *The Book* to her chest like a breastplate. "To my mind, that's what *The Book of the Wys* was suggesting I do."

"The man surely isn't fool enough to test me," Thien said.

"He's run through his wife's money, and he's afraid of no longer being rich," Adrya said, making Thien raise an eyebrow. I was startled too, and I was willing to bet that Dugan didn't know about any money troubles. "Fear can make people do things they otherwise wouldn't."

Thien ran his little finger around the inside of a tight shirt cuff. After he was shot in the autumn, he'd been thinner for a while. It looked like he was building up muscle again. Thien was not a man to let himself go soft. "Keep me informed." He turned to leave, and I was moving toward the door when he swung back and squared off on me. I froze the same way Rosin had done in the Hall.

"What's this I hear about you begging money off Lady Lineth to run a refuge for homeless children?" Thien asked.

I peeled my dry tongue off the roof of my mouth. "Lady Lineth runs it, Your Majesty." I glanced behind me as if the door might have closed, trapping me in this small room.

"But you asked her to do it," Thien said.

Behind him, Adrya frowned at me. *Surprise, Adrya!* "Not exactly, sir. She asked me what it had been like to live in the streets, and I told her. She asked if many kids lived that way, and when I said they did, she said she wanted to help."

"She's my ward," Thien said. "I'm responsible for seeing that her money isn't thrown away."

"She's a smart woman, sir. She runs it herself. No one's cheating her."

Thien's eyes bored into me. Finally he nodded. "Just remember I see her accounts." He swept from the room, which suddenly felt like it had more air.

"You didn't ask my permission to set up this orphanage." Adrya scowled at me.

"Like I said, Lady Lineth set it up. I just helped when she asked me to. Besides, I didn't think I needed to ask permission." That wasn't quite true. I'd been afraid Adrya would tell me not to waste my time on work she hadn't given me, so I'd carefully kept her ignorant and happy. "It's the kind of thing a Wysman is supposed to do. I mean, you just read a passage about how adults should care for children." She opened her mouth to say more, but I got there first. "So I'm going to my cousin's, remember?" I turned toward escape.

"Oh, very well. Don't dawdle though," Adrya called after me. "I'll expect you in the library as soon as you're back."

RELIEVED TO BE on my way at last, I hustled out into the back hallway where I nearly ran into a tall young woman with shiny dark hair who stepped out of the shadows. I rocked to a halt and bit back my impatience. "Beg pardon, Lady Lineth. Did you need me?"

Lady Lineth's cheeks were paler than usual, which probably meant she'd overheard Thien and me talking about her. The lack of color didn't make her any less pretty though. Anyone should be able to see why Prince Beran was in love with her. It was her tragedy that her father was the one who'd tried to assassinate King Thien. Lineth was only three years older than me, and already her life was spoiled. If Beran had ever hoped his father would let him marry Lineth, that hope must be gone now, despite the fortune she'd inherited from her mother. I had no idea if Thien had ever hit his son, but I knew he was willing to cause him pain if he thought it would strengthen the kingdom.

"I'm sorry to bother you, Jarka," Lineth said. "I heard you say you're going to your cousin's, but two of the children are missing from the refuge."

All my wandering attention snapped to her. "How long have they been gone?"

"Ellyn says they were there when everyone got up, so only an hour or so."

"Who is it?"

"Rena and Laren," Lineth said.

"What happened? Was someone after them? Family, maybe, or some pimp?"

She didn't flinch at "pimp" or the idea that family showing up could be bad. She'd learned a lot in the last few months. "Ellyn was pretty frantic, but she and Tally both think they ran away. One of them had a bad dream that frightened them. They were talking about the Grabber."

My fears took a quick crooked turn. This, not Lyssa, must be what the wind was warning me about. The tension that had churned in my gut since I read the wind eased a little. Rena and Laren had been fine an hour ago, and they probably weren't in much danger yet. It was, after all, broad daylight and people were astir with shopping and business. They ran because they were small enough to still believe in a fright tale, not because someone was after them. The kids in the refuge were easily spooked. I didn't blame them. Sleeping alone in the streets does that to you, and I'd brought Rena and her little brother to the refuge only two weeks earlier.

"I'll look for them. If they didn't get lost along the way, they probably went back more or less to the place where I found them. Who's Ellyn?"

"I hired her to work with Tally during the day and sleep there at night," Lineth said. "She heard I was looking for someone and came to see me. She's the oldest of eight children, so I thought she'd know how to manage them at night. His Majesty has made it clear I have to sleep in the castle." She nodded toward the room I'd just come from.

"If she's lost two kids already, Ellyn may be learning street kids are harder to manage than her brothers and sisters. What were she and Tally doing that Rena and Laren just walked away?"

"They were busy feeding, washing, and dressing all of them. It's harder than you think, Jarka." She waited to see if I'd protest, but now that she mentioned it, I had memories of how slippery Izzy had been as a toddler. "You'll like her," Lineth finally went on. "One reason I hired her was she reminded me a little of you."

I pictured a skinny girl with one good leg, her dark hair sticking out in clumps over her ears because the castle barber had given up. "Charming, you mean?" We started walking toward the door leading out into the courtyard.

"She loves books," Lineth said. "I told her you did too."

"A surefire way to impress a girl," I said. I'd never yet met one who didn't prefer a man with two good feet.

She laughed and surrendered the argument. "Thank you for going after Rena and Laren. I didn't know who else to ask."

"They're probably fine." The vision from my wind box flickered through my head, but I kept it to myself. I nodded farewell to Lineth and slipped past her toward the door. Experience had taught me that events in a vision could be changed, but given that blank moment, it would be best if I hurried.

# Chapter 3

WITH PRAYERS OVER, the courtyard had come alive. I snagged three rolls from the kitchens and, shaking my rapped knuckles, dodged around a group of young men who were sharing jokes as they drew on their riding gloves. Their fur-trimmed cloaks were probably making them sweat, but they did draw admiring looks from the three pretty girls coming out of the castle to join them. The girls skirted around me without even looking at me. It wasn't the worst reaction I'd ever had from a girl. I'd say it was their loss except I seemed to be the one missing out.

At the gate from the castle to the city street, a grocer struggled to maneuver a cart of vegetables around the tight corner. Munching on the first roll, I squeezed between the cart and the gate and set off down the steeply slanting Kings Way, which ran from the castle at the city's highest point down to New Square. I'd found Rena and Laren behind an ale house not far away near the city's South Gate, the part of town where country folks often lived when they came seeking a better life in Rin. More fools they. Not that I wanted to live in the country—the Powers save me—but the country folks were so trusting, they were nearly as helpless as Rena and Laren. The smell of clean air that clung to them attracted every thief and thug in the city.

Kings Way brightened as the sun spilled over the peaks of the thatched roofs and fell into the valleys of the streets. I hitched along as speedily as I could, keeping to the edge so as to stay out of the way of the servants and housewives running errands. When I reached New Square, I paused, scanning the ends of the two most likely streets Rena and Laren would have taken. My gaze caught on a familiar figure tossing pebbles into the fountain at the spot where kids who worked as messengers waited for customers. I circled the fountain toward him. A Darklight wheel already spun in the falling water, endlessly lifting and dropping the four figures: the man, the woman, the baby, the crone.

"Hey, Timur." Smiling at the ragged boy seated on the marble lip of the lowest pool, I perched next to him. It felt astonishingly good to be with someone I'd known forever.

"What are you doing here?" Timur flicked a jagged fingernail against the black linen of my shirt. "What a gent you're getting to be."

Timur grinned when he said it, but I was suddenly

conscious of the way a shabby serving maid had just skirted around me. I felt my smile fade.

"You still scamming them up at the castle with that box of yours?" Timur asked.

I'd always told friends I couldn't really read the wind. I'd been afraid powerful people would hear of my gift and take me away from Lyssa. I was just a kid, of course, and my mother had died, so I was big on staying where I was. There's a joke in there somewhere, one that's on me. "I read the wind for them when they let me."

Timur laughed. "You never let up, do you? Good for you."

I decided there was no point in arguing. Life had stripped Timur of easy trust even in a fellow street kid. Maybe *especially* in a fellow street kid. He knew what we could be driven to. What's more, he didn't feel the elements' energy throbbing under his feet. I thought again that I lived in a different city than most people. "You been here all morning?"

"Since dawn." Timur sniffled, sucking a drop of snot back into his nose. "I'm having a lean time. Everyone's been hired but me."

"You seen a boy and a girl? Him about three, her maybe six? They'd have come down Kings Way and been through here soon after light."

"She has skinny braids sticking out sideways?" Timur pointed to the most westerly street leading from the square. "They went that way. I wondered what they were doing out on their own."

I heaved myself to my feet. "They ran away from Lady Lineth's refuge because one of them had a nightmare about the Grabber."

He laughed. "They do say the Grabber lives in the castle. When I was a kid, my granny said she'd leave me there if I didn't behave." He waved his arms menacingly. "Ooga booga. You better be careful, Jarka."

"Thanks for the warning," I said wryly. I gave him my last roll and plunged into a street lined with cobblers and leather goods shops. I'd gone only a few blocks when the buzz of tight voices made me glance down a narrow side street. A group of people had gathered around a man who was crouching to look at something on the ground. As I looked, he stood and I glimpsed a slender body sprawled on the cobbles. My heart stopped, then thundered as I hurried toward them. I was too late. I'd wasted time arguing with Dugan and waiting on Adrya and Thien, and now Rena or Laren had paid the price.

The man whose back had blocked my vision moved aside, and I realized the kid on the ground was too big to be Rena or Laren. I sagged onto my crutch, then went closer to see who it was. A boy of maybe twelve or thirteen lay on his back, his eyes half closed. I recognized him though I didn't know his name. Like Timur, he was a messenger, and I'd seen him both by the fountain and at the castle.

"What happened to him?" I asked.

The man who'd been crouching glanced at me. "Knocked the back of his head on the cobbles hard enough to crack his skull." He pointed to where flies buzzed over a puddle of dried blood at the street's edge.

"He didn't fall on his own," a woman said. "I heard a scuffle out here in the night, and when I peeked out through the shutters, I saw a man running away. I didn't see this one though." She nodded, sober-faced, at the body. "Not in the dark and shoved up against the house wall."

I stared down at the nameless boy. His face and body were unmarred, and yet he was so undeniably dead, so full of absence, I was sure this must be what the wind meant to show me this morning. But how did that make sense? That vision should have been for me, and I'd never even spoken to this boy. I swayed a little on my crutch, thinking hard. Could his death connect to my concerns in some other way? I couldn't see how. He wasn't even a kid I could have taken to the refuge. He was too old.

At the thought of the refuge, I remembered Rena and Laren. I tore my gaze from the dead kid, hustled back to the street I'd been on, and started off south again. If this boy was my responsibility, I didn't know what to do about it, but I *did* know what to do about Rena and Laren. Given what happened to the boy, I needed to move my arse and do it.

Tradesmen's houses gave way to shabby huts where laborers collapsed into exhausted sleep every night. Some of the cobblestones were loose or missing here, and I had to pick my way through them like I did through Dugan's dropped clothes. Garbage reeked in the gutters strongly enough to make my eyes water. I breathed through my mouth.

Even before I rounded the corner to the back of the Sleeping Dog alehouse, I heard a thin, high-pitched voice singing the tale of the frog and the grasshopper. *Thank the Powers.* The dead boy faded from my head, and I followed the wavering notes to a hidey hole between a rain barrel and the alehouse's back steps. I dodged a scurrying rat, then leaned over the barrel to look down at the two sitting cross-legged with their backs against the alehouse wall. My shadow fell on them, and they both screamed.

"Good," I said. "You should be scared. Do you know how stupid you were to run away? Come out of there."

Rena scowled up at me and put her arm around Laren. "Go away, Jarka."

I caught myself getting ready to cut loose on her with sharp words that would be better aimed at the adults— including me—who were supposed to be caring for her. Besides, I already knew she wasn't a kid who'd be easy to push around, which was mostly a good thing. "You planning to stay here? What'll you do when it rains?"

"Get wet." Rena's voice was defiant.

"I hear there's a new refuge mistress. Ellyn, I think? She's worried about you. Why don't you let me take you back?"

Rena shook her head hard enough that Laren had to duck away from the slap of her braids. "The Grabber is there." She sounded breathless with fear.

"The Grabber is just a fright tale."

"He's not," Rena said. "I saw him."

"Saw him." Laren nodded, his eyes round.

"You were dreaming," I said.

Rena shook her head again. Laren glanced at her and echoed the motion.

"It's warm at the refuge," I said, "and I'll bet there's something good to eat. What are you planning to have here?"

"What?" Laren asked Rena trustingly.

I found myself wondering what it would be like to trust and love someone so completely. I faintly recalled feeling that way about my mother before she died and then, in a faded way, about Lyssa. But I dumped all that when I decided it was time to grow up and look after myself.

Rena chewed her lip and must have found it poor eating. "If the Grabber wasn't there, we could go." She cocked her head at me and spoke doubtfully. "Maybe you could chase him away?"

"Sure. I'll tell him to beat it."

She pursed her lips, gave a sharp nod, and rose, drawing Laren to his feet. They edged around the barrel and stood waiting, hand in hand.

I jerked my head toward the castle, high on the hill.

"Let's go then. I want to stop somewhere on the way." I shepherded the two kids through narrow streets and then wider ones, with the image of the dead boy floating to the surface of my head again. Why had the wind shown him to me? A warning maybe, but of what? I felt like I'd failed him, like I owed him something. The best I could think of to do was warn Lyssa that a kid killer was on the loose.

When we turned into Tailors Lane, I expected to see Lyssa dealing with customers over the counter in her window. But the shutter was up, and no one answered my knock.

"What do you want?" Clovyan's voice boomed down the street.

Rena flung her arm across Laren's chest and slammed him against the next-door-neighbor's house. I whirled, my heart thudding like an alarm drum. Clovyan loomed an arm's length away, which was a yard too close for comfort. A curl of his dark hair fell across his high forehead. His shirt fit with easy grace, a tribute to his trade as a tailor. "Did Lyssa send for you? I warned her not to."

I glimpsed Laren's eyes growing huge before Rena hunched over him, shielding him from view. I feared my own eyes might be bigger than usual too. "A kid was killed not far from here last night. You shouldn't let Izzy wander on her own."

"Keep your nose out of what Izzy does," Clovyan said. "We don't need your advice."

"I'm just telling you what happened."

"So now you've told me and can get your sorry arse out of here."

My whole body twitched with the urge to scurry out of his sight as fast as I could. I had to fight to force out words. "When will Lyssa be back? I have a Darklight gift for Izzy."

"Give it to me." Clovyan extended a huge hand.

I blinked at it. Clovyan's hands looked readier to knock someone down than to sew a seam in delicate fabric, though I'd seen—or felt—him do both. I could barely breathe. There was no way I could force myself close enough to that hand to put candy in it. "I'll come back and give it to her myself."

"You afraid I'm going to steal it? Is that what you think of honest tradesmen now you're up there in the castle?" Clovyan leaned in, and I couldn't stop myself from backing away. My hand slipped on the crutch, and I realized my palm was slick with sweat.

"I haven't changed my opinion of you at all," I said.

"Who do you think you're fooling anyway? You're no Wysman. You're a lazy liar who thinks he's too good for the place the Powers made for him. You may take tea with the king, but in my own house, I'm the king, and I'm telling you to stay away unless you're after another beating." He pushed me out of his way, leaving me scrambling to regain my balance as he stalked inside and slammed the door. Even after he'd gone in, my heart still pounded. I teetered between relief and self-loathing that I couldn't shake the terror of that beating even with the door between us, no matter how much time had passed.

"My wind box still says you'll end up in jail, Clovyan," I shouted. *Oh yeah*, jeered a voice in my head. *Very brave now that he's on the other side of a closed door.* The neighbor peeked out her front door. Face burning, I turned to find that Rena hadn't moved. "Come on." She lifted her head cautiously. "Come on," I said more gently. "Let's get you back to the refuge where someone can keep an eye on you."

Rena darted a look at Clovyan's door, then seized Laren's hand and ran around the next corner, dragging him after her. At least she had a good sense of danger, though she seemed to think it would mostly fall on Laren, a fact that suggested she'd seen things I didn't want to think about.

I followed her, not looking back. If Clovyan came charging after us, I'd soon know it. *Lyssa, Lyssa, why can't you smarten up?* I herded Rena and Laren toward Kings Way. Gradually, my heart slowed to normal.

"That man was stupid," Rena said. "He doesn't know you can make scary things go away."

I had to grin. To Rena, I wasn't just some kid with a bad foot who could be pushed around, no matter what Clovyan or Dugan or some unshakeable part of me thought. I was a man with a gift, someone who would take care of her. "So what do you think of Miss Ellyn?" I asked her. No harm checking that Lineth had made a good choice. "She's not why you ran away, is she?"

Rena shook her head, her braids whipping up a breeze. "She knows how to tuck you in at night."

As a recommendation, I'd heard worse.

At the top of the hill, we turned and followed the street running along the castle wall, making our way toward a row of small houses built right up against the castle. The door stood open on the first one, and high-pitched voices rolled out and bounced down the cobblestone street. Rena held Laren back as I climbed the single step and peeked in to see a dozen boys and girls seated around the table, bent over their slates.

The boy nearest the door looked up. He'd been half feral when I cornered him in an abandoned shed. Now he was doing sums. He leapt from his chair. "Jarka! The Grabber took Rena and Laren."

"No, he didn't, stupid." A taller girl jumped up to join in. "Miss Ellyn says it was a bad dream." They all crowded in front of me, gabbling out their news.

"But Rena saw him, and now they're gone."

"No, they're not." I beckoned to Rena, who still held Laren back from entering.

"Oh, thank the Powers." A girl about my own age pushed through the crowd of kids and ran out to crouch and fling one arm around Rena's shoulders and the other around Laren's. She closed her eyes for a moment, looking deeply relieved. She'd been knitting something blue, and it flapped in Laren's face. He sneezed and batted it away.

She turned her face up toward me, and I found myself

looking into toffee-brown eyes. Her dark hair sprang out in a bush of curls she'd tried and failed to tame with a red ribbon. "I can't thank you enough for retrieving them." Her smile felt like sunshine warming my back. I tried to think of the last time a girl smiled at me like that and came up with never. She straightened but kept one hand on Rena's shoulder and one on Laren's, telling me she'd already learned they could be slippery. As she stood, her skirt fell straight, and I realized she wore a knife on her belt. Not a dainty one like ladies used for cutting embroidery thread. A big one meant to serve as a weapon. A jolt of power seemed to leap from that knife right into my gut. She must be fiercer than she looked. I should introduce her to Lyssa.

I realized I was staring at her hip and dragged my eyes away to glare at Rena. "They're brats, but they know better than to run away again, don't they?" She stuck out her lower lip.

"I should have kept a better eye on them." The girl tossed her head to dislodge a wind-blown curl without letting go of Rena and Laren. Even that small move was graceful. I was so used to my crutch I didn't usually think about it. I thought of it now. "You must be Jarka. Lady Lineth tells me you helped her establish the refuge. You've done a good thing."

"And you must be Ellyn." My tongue trembled with the desire to tell her I was also Wyswoman Adrya's apprentice, but for once the Powers were merciful and my mouth had gone too dry to speak.

She took Laren's hand and pressed Rena toward the door of the refuge. "Come inside."

"Not yet." Rena planted her feet. "Jarka has to chase the Grabber away."

Ellyn raised an eyebrow at me.

For a moment, I considered backing out of my promise to Rena, but she and Laren both regarded me trustingly. Life had already done everything it could to break their faith in the world. I wasn't going to be the one to finally make it happen. "I have to tell him to leave," I told Ellyn. Heat flamed in my face. Oh yeah, she was sure to see me as a Wysman now even without my telling her.

With a broad smile, she waved toward the door. "Go to it."

Aware she was watching my awkwardness, I clumped into the refuge, where I found Lady Lineth sitting at the table in the room's center, presiding over the day's lessons. "Bless you, Jarka," she said. "I knew you'd find them."

"I told Rena I'd chase the Grabber away." It sounded defensive even to my own ears, but Lineth just nodded. I glanced over my shoulder to see Ellyn, Rena, and Laren on the doorstep. Ellyn was still smiling, but Rena and Laren watched me soberly. Fine. I'd do it and be done. I swept my gaze over the refuge. "Get out of here, Grabber. There." I crooked my finger at Rena.

She shook her head. "Not scary enough. Use your wind."

"What?" Ellyn sounded amused.

"Jarka's a wind reader," Lady Lineth said.

"You didn't tell me that," Ellyn said. Even from where I stood, I saw her whole body stiffen.

Lovely. Everything about Ellyn's face and stance told me she thought like the guard who'd been on the walkway this morning. She was no longer merely amused at my expense. She thought I was messing about with evil and unnatural forces. I turned back to the room. I knew better than to believe I could change her mind, and given that, I might as well go the whole hog.

"Come and sit down, children," Lineth said. "Get out of Jarka's way. There'll be power on the loose." They scrambled to obey, then sat with their gazes tied tight to me. I decided I preferred being scary to being ridiculous.

I drew a breath and raised my free hand. "Grabber, Grabber, hear me." I made my way along the row of cots against the scarred stones of the castle wall that formed the refuge's fourth side. I waved my hand in what I hoped looked like a magical sign over each bed. "If you ever come into this place again, I'll kick your backside and pound you into jelly."

I rounded the far end of the room near the hearth. A door stood open on a room with two narrow beds and a writing table. Lady Lineth had shared it with Tally, so Ellyn probably lived there now. Something white lay neatly folded on each pillow. I recognized nightgowns. I didn't go in. If the Grabber was there, Ellyn was going to have to take care of herself. With that knife. In her nightgown. An unexpected thrill ran through me at the thought.

*Wrong*, squeaked a voice in my heard. *Very, very wrong. Besides, she thinks you're meddling with evil.*

I started back down the line of cots, every head in the place swiveling to watch me. "Get out and stay out, Grabber, because I tell you, I'm tough, but these kids are tougher. If you think I'm scary, wait until *they* come after you." From the corner of my eye, I saw several kids sit straighter, and a girl made her hands into fists.

Back in the doorway, I ignored Ellyn. She wasn't the first girl who'd ever scorned me. "How's that?" I asked Rena.

"My bed." Rena pointed to a cot.

I thrust my arm out toward it. "And especially stay away from Rena."

"And Laren," Rena said.

"And Laren," I echoed.

Rena let out a long breath. "All right." She came into the house, Laren's hand in hers. Lineth rose to greet them, but she was watching me and Ellyn.

"Thank you," Ellyn murmured rather stiffly.

"Yes. Thank you for the show," drawled an unfortunately familiar voice, and I looked behind Ellyn to see Dugan in the street with both his parents.

# Chapter 4

L ADY LINETH ROSE, head up and shoulders back in the Gracious Lady posture I'd seen her use before when she courted rich folks for donations. The children around the table blinked and leaned back in their chairs at their teacher's transformation. "Lord Rosin, Lady Brylla, thank you for visiting the refuge."

"Of course, my dear." Rosin of Stonebridge Manor led his wife into the room, though Dugan just peeked around the doorway before drawing back out of sight like he didn't want to be seen with his parents. "We couldn't stay away once you described the wonderful work being done here and its need for patrons." He took the hand Lineth offered, bent over it, and at the last moment, turned it palm upwards to kiss. He held on a good three heartbeats longer than was polite, and I could see Lineth tugging on it. Lady Brylla's eyes narrowed.

Once again, I was struck by how young Rosin was

compared to his wife. His skin was smooth and his belly flat while her cheeks drooped and gray showed at her temples.

"Lord and lady, this is Ellyn, one of the refuge mistresses," Lineth told Rosin. I glimpsed her wiping her palm on the side of her skirt away from him. "And perhaps you already know Jarka? He's Wyswoman Adrya's apprentice and, I believe, Dugan's roommate."

The look Lady Brylla gave me nearly blasted me off my feet. "We've not met, but anyone could see what a *fine* Wysman he'd make based on that show with the Grabber." She crouched in front of Rena. "What's your name, sweetheart?" she cooed. "You're too big to believe in the Grabber, aren't you? Not like silly Jarka."

Rena eyed her warily. "I saw him."

"Now, now. I'll bet you can't even tell me what he looked like."

"He was big. Like the Grabber. He smelled like flowers."

"Flowers?" Brylla shook her head. "I don't think you really saw him."

"It was dark." Rena crossed her arms over her scrawny chest. "I screamed, and I scared him, and he ran away."

"Scared him," Laren echoed with a nod.

Chuckling, Brylla tried to pat Laren's cheek, but he scrambled out of her reach, leaving her with her hand out, patting thin air. She pretended she'd meant to smooth her skirt as she rose and turned to Lineth, who was edging away from Lord Rosin. "Lineth, perhaps you didn't know that Dugan expected to be given that apprentice's place with Adrya. That's why we allowed him to come to Rin City when His Majesty sent for him."

"I believe Prince Beran was the one who saw Jarka's talent. Although I'm sure Dugan is talented too in his own way." I knew Lineth pretty well by now, and I heard the ice in her voice, even if Dugan's horrible parents didn't seem to. Lineth was good at the subtle ways I'd seen court folks slip a verbal shiv into one another.

"He certainly is," Lady Brylla said. "My husband's family descends directly from the Wys Ones. Wisdom and the power it brings run in our family. Dugan has inherited it all."

Wisdom? Dugan? The only power I'd ever seen him show came from his fists.

"Come inside, Dugan. Greet Lady Lineth." Brylla snapped her fingers.

Dugan flushed but did as he was told, bowing to Lineth and taking her hand. At least he didn't slobber over it as his father had done. Looking annoyed, Rosin elbowed his son aside.

What charming people. I considered paying them the courtesy of a farewell but decided they'd just ignore me anyway. Since Dugan and I had last spoken when I whacked him with my crutch, I sure as spit had nothing courteous to say to him. Instead, I turned to Ellyn. "Ellyn, I'm glad to have met you." My eye caught on her knife. To my own surprise, I heard myself add, "I hope we meet again."

She backed a tiny step away. "Thank you again for finding Rena and Laren."

Stone it. I was too stupid to realize when I wasn't wanted. But then, I already knew that.

I glimpsed Dugan's gaze darting from me to Ellyn. Abandoning Lineth to his father, he closed in on her. In a voice I'd certainly never heard him use, he said, "You're so generous to work with the children. They must be a handful."

Ellyn smoothed Laren's hair. "We owe them our care and protection," she said.

"I couldn't agree more," Dugan said.

I thumped out of the house and back along the street, uncertain whether I preferred being the fraud Timur saw or the menace Ellyn did. In neither case was I someone to be valued for what he could do. I didn't care. As long as Prince Beran valued it, the wind and I would do just fine together.

The dead boy's blank face drifted through my head. *Do just fine at what?* whispered the voice. *Can you figure out what the wind wants? If not, maybe everyone else is right, and you're really not worth having around.*

I WAS NEARLY to the castle gate when I heard a light step

hurrying after me. For a stupid moment, I pictured Ellyn, but when I turned, Lineth was right behind me. "Tally's back from the market. If you're going to the castle, may I walk with you?" She took my arm, and fury at Dugan seeped out of my body. I couldn't remember a woman ever taking my arm before. A crutch didn't exactly encourage them to rely on me. I tried to keep my step even.

"Both of them are rude and patronizing, and he's a womanizer," she said in a voice pitched for my ears only. "But the refuge needs an endowment to give it a reliable income, and Rosin hinted he might donate."

I considered telling her that Adrya said Dugan's family needed money, but I wasn't supposed to share what Adrya and the king talked about. Another thought made me stiffen. "Are you thinking of withdrawing your support?" I remembered the conversation in the king's waiting room. "Would Thien make you do that?"

She fingered the charm she wore on a thin silver chain around her neck. From glimpses I'd had, I knew it was a love knot, and I was pretty sure I knew who'd given it to her. "I have to believe the king is more generous than that. It's just that I'm not sure where I'll be living in the long run."

I hesitated long enough to think better of it, but stuck my nose in anyway. "Maybe when Beran comes home, he'll settle that."

"Has His Majesty had word of when to expect him?"

she asked.

"Not that I know of."

She tucked the charm inside her gown. After a silent moment, she looked up at me from the corner of her eye. "Are you going to the dancing tonight?"

"I wasn't planning to."

"You should."

For the second time in an hour, I thought about my foot. "Lady, I use a crutch." I felt ridiculous pointing out the obvious. Lineth wasn't stupid. What was this about?

"You probably dance as well as some men I've had for partners."

"Are you going?" I asked. As far as I knew, she'd stopped going to castle gatherings after her father's treason and death.

She was silent as we passed between the two guards at the castle gate, both of whom drew slightly away. Her hand tightened on my arm. One corner of her mouth lifted. "You need to be careful, Jarka," she whispered a little shakily. "You might be contaminated by the traitor's daughter."

"I'm willing to take the risk." I had a sudden, vivid memory of my mother telling me my crooked foot was a gift from the Powers, a challenge that would make me a deeper person who saw the world more truly. The old legends said a mark like my foot was the reason I could read the wind, compensation from the Powers for what they'd withheld. I wondered if I could persuade Lineth to see her father's treachery as a gift. It was a gift for the kids at the refuge, for sure.

"I'll go to the dancing if you promise to go too," Lineth said. "I need to know I'll see a friendly face."

I guessed the guards' shunning had hurt her more than she let on. "All right." I owed Lineth, and it wasn't a lot to ask. I'd sit and keep her company.

She drummed her fingers on my arm, then said, "I freed Ellyn from her duties tonight so she could go."

I snorted. "Matchmaking, lady?" I had a flash of an image of me holding that fierce, agile girl in my arms. I swallowed a sharp pain of longing. "You need to study your targets better. Judging by how she reacted to my being a wind reader, Ellyn is one of the people who fears wind reading, or channeling any other element, too. She probably calls it sorcery when I'm not around."

"That's not because of you. Ellyn told me the story of it in case it put me off hiring her. A number of years ago, her little brother disappeared. Ellyn was supposed to be watching him though she couldn't have been much older than Rena. Eventually they found his body dumped in a gutter. They had trouble making sure it was him because his body was oddly shriveled, like a little old man's. Ellyn's family said it had to be sorcery. That's their word, Jarka, not mine. I know that's not what you do, and once she gets to know you, she'll see you channel the wind's knowledge to help Beran be more aware of people who don't live in the castle." Her voice quivered only a little when she said the prince's name.

"The elements are wild," honesty forced me to admit. "If someone wanted to use them to do harm, or maybe was just inept, they could do bad things." A puff of wind fluttered the strands of hair on my forehead, and I recalled the dead boy. He'd died from a blow on the head, an ordinary bad thing, not misused elemental power. But the wind had more or less put his death in my care. If only it had shown me what to *do* about it. "A boy was killed in the streets last night. Ellyn and Tally might want to keep an extra eye out for trouble."

Lineth made a soft, distressed sound. I held the door for her as we entered the castle, and she was reaching for my arm again when the sound of a hurrying step made us both turn, and a breathless Lord Rosin caught up to us. He swept an elaborate bow, looking pleased as a cat who'd found the cream unguarded. There was no sign of Dugan or Brylla. They must still be at the refuge. Where fierce Ellyn was. Not that it mattered to me.

"Lady Lineth, I'm happy to have run into you."

"Run" was the telling word, I thought. Rosin was panting from his haste.

"I'm told Thien has a painting by Nica the Dolyan, but I keep losing my way when I try to find it." Rosin held out his arm. "I beg you to be merciful enough to show me the way lest I wander these halls forever." He might claim to be begging, but he sounded confident enough to me. Of course, I wasn't the one he was talking to. I wasn't even sure he saw me.

Lineth was silent for an instant longer than was polite before putting her hand on his arm rather than mine. "I'd be happy to." She gave me an apologetic look. "Thank you, Jarka. This way, sir." She steered Rosin into a side hallway.

As they set off, Rosin said, "What's this I hear about you being married soon?"

I stared after them. Was this what Lineth had been thinking about when she said she wasn't sure where she'd wind up?

As they rounded the corner, Lineth said, "I promise you I have no plans to marry."

I relaxed for the refuge's sake, but I was still offended at Rosin prying into something I knew caused Lineth pain. I'd seen her with Prince Beran. When the two of them were together, they leaned slightly toward one another, like plants bending toward the sun. I still didn't understand how King Thien could stand in the way of his son's happiness. Adrya had told me more than once that a king made hard choices, and as a Wysman, I'd have to advise him how to serve Rinland, not just his family. That was responsible use of power, she said.

The thought of Adrya made relief wash through me. She'd be waiting in the library, where the mysteries to be unraveled were of words and wisdom.

ADRYA LOOKED UP from the scroll on the library table. "Is your cousin all right?" I nodded. No point going into details. Adrya nodded at the stool across from her, and I lowered myself onto it. "Go on with your translation."

While she went back to studying her scroll, I pushed worries about the outside world aside and opened the book of folk tales I'd been working on the day before. They were not only in the Wys Ones' old language, but also recorded in their runes. I was supposed to be working my way up to translating an original copy of *The Book of the Wys*. I reread what I'd left chalked on my slate the day before: "The little lost fawn ran up to the squirrel. 'Have you seen my mama? I am lost and need someone to care for me.'" I worked for a while on the rest of the story. This being a tale, not real life, the fawn found its mother in the end. The kids in the refuge would probably like this story, I thought. They'd need one in modern script, though, and in Rinnish. *Ellyn would like it too*, whispered a voice in my head. *Lineth said she liked books*. I pushed my slate across the table for Adrya to check. She raised a finger for me to wait until she finished what she was reading. I twirled my chalk, eyeing the shelves of books. Until I became Adrya's apprentice, I'd never seen so many in one place. There were days when I dithered trying to choose one to read because picking one meant not picking another.

"Adrya, would it be all right if I borrowed a book of folk tales for Lady Lineth's refuge?"

"What?" She looked up, a finger marking her place,

obviously irritated that I'd interrupted her train of thought. I repeated my request. "One of the castle's books? Of course not. Street urchins would destroy it."

"They wouldn't. Someone would read it to them, Lady Lineth or one of the refuge mistresses, and you know they'd be careful."

As I talked, she kept flicking her gaze down to the scroll. For a moment, she acted as if she hadn't heard me.

"Adrya?" I prompted.

"Oh, all right. If harm comes to it, you'll bear the blame." She dove back into her scroll.

I went to the bookcase holding folk tales, took a moment to inhale their dusty smell, and pulled one out at random. I was leafing through it, looking for the tale I'd just translated, when a title caught my eye: "The Tale of the Grabber." My skin prickled. I'd never seen a written version of the Grabber story. I hadn't even heard anyone talk about him in years, and yet today, the story leapt at me from all sides. *It's a coincidence*, I told myself sternly. Nonetheless, I held my breath as I read.

> *In the time of times, two women lived near the sacred place on the hill by the great river. One had a son of four years, blithe and dear to her heart. The other had a son of the same age, but she was busy with her own tasks and had no time for him.*
>
> *It happened that on a day, the children played together while their mothers picked blackberries. When the mothers looked up, they saw only wind*

in the grass.

"Ah! Ah!" said the first. "Where is my boy? Come now and help me find him."

The other shrugged. "They have but wandered off. My husband is waiting for his berries. I will search when I have fed him."

But the first would not wait. She searched the bushes and the brambles, and behind a stand of hawthorn, she found a cave. Her heart beat like the wings of a bird in a snare, but she knew her child was there, and so she entered. She stumbled through the dark, until ahead of her, she heard the sound of falling water. She crept forward and stood at the edge of a stone room. In the room was a well, and next to it stood a creature of evil, holding her son, ready to drop him in the water.

At the sight of her child in danger, courage roared within her. She lunged at the evil one, who saw at once that the mother's love was stronger than the creature's desire to steal what the child had—youth and health and life yet to come. The creature dropped the child and fled. The mother took the boy in her trembling arms and carried him home.

But when the other mother heard of the cave and went to search it, her child was not there. She looked and looked, but she was too late. She never saw her child again.

More uneasy than I wanted to admit, I stared at the tale's last words. I couldn't help but think the Powers had laid yet another dead or missing child in my path, daring me to figure out what to do. *It's only a tale*, I told myself. *You're not Rena's age.* Still, I slid the book back into its place. Given the way the kids were all stirred up about the Grabber, I'd do better to find a collection of stories without this one.

I paged through two other books and decided the second one would be good. As I was turning to carry it back to the table, I noticed a thin book slightly tilted out from the others. When I tried to push it back into line, what felt like a spark jumped from it to my finger. I stifled a cry and stuck my finger in my mouth.

"What is it?" Adrya looked up.

"I don't know." I hesitated, then tugged my sleeve over my hand and pulled the book from the shelf. The cover showed only a stone arch like a gateway. Even through a layer of cloth, the thing pulsed with elemental power. Not a kind of power I'd willingly channel though. My stomach turned over, but I let the book fall open in my palm. What looked like a poem or an incantation filled the page. "For the Well of Sharing" read the line at the top.

A hand reached into my line of vision and snatched the book away. I hadn't even heard Adrya approach. "Where did you get that?" She snapped the book shut.

"It was here." I pointed to the shelf of tales, then gulped a deep breath. I was unexpectedly dizzy.

"That's not where it belongs," she said. "Who moved it?"

"Not me."

She hustled to a corner, nudged a step stool into place, and climbed up to put the book on one of the high shelves full of books she'd said were collected from elsewhere. I'd always assumed they were foreign, but the book I'd touched was in Rinnish. Adrya brushed her hands together as she climbed down.

"Did you feel some power from it?" I asked.

"Don't be ridiculous."

"What's it about?" I asked.

"Not for you yet," she said. "Come. We'll see how well you did with your translation."

Taking the book I'd decided would do for the refuge, I followed her back to the table. That other book had felt dangerous. So did it make me a better Wysman or a worse one that it responded to me and I to it?

LATE THAT AFTERNOON, I was approaching my room when the curtain slid aside, and a big man in unfamiliar livery came out with a clothes chest on his shoulder. I flattened myself in the nook next to the fireplace to let him by. I had just straightened again when Dugan followed the man out of our room.

"Careful with that," Dugan called. The man grunted

and kept going.

"You leaving?" I tried not to sound delighted. Dugan might change his mind to spite me.

Dugan gave a self-satisfied smile. "Not that it's any of your business, but my parents want me to stay with them while they're here. They don't think it's right for me to be thrown in with dirt like you. They're so disgusted, they might even take me home with them when they go."

"I'd be disgusted if I were your family, too." I brushed past him, then looked over my shoulder to grin at him.

"That Ellyn is pretty," Dugan said. "I invited her to meet me at the dancing tonight." He turned to follow the serving man.

My hand tightened on the book of tales. I was a fool. That much was clear because I still meant to go to the dancing. *It's for Lineth*, I told myself. In the back of my head, a voice sneered, *Sure it is.*

# Chapter 5

*D*ANCING, I THOUGHT sourly as I limped from pool to pool of lantern light along the castle corridor. *Right.* From the Great Hall, music and the thud of feet swelled and faded as the hallway doubled back on itself before dumping me into the antechamber. I hovered in the shadows at the end of the corridor, watching a handful of castle folks and visitors talking and laughing in the cool air sweeping in through the open courtyard doors. I'd never gone into the Great Hall when dancing was underway. As I'd told Lady Lineth, dancing wasn't my best thing. Truth be told, it wasn't my *any* thing. I preferred not to make a fool of myself in public, thank you very much. I'd sometimes sat outside in the courtyard, though, listening to the music. It sounded clearly enough there that couples often came out to dance and maybe slip away into the dark, too. I fought off the temptation to go out and sit by myself in the dark now. I'd promised Lineth. Besides, as she'd said, if I wanted Ellyn to warm up to me—defying every experience I'd ever had with a girl, I seemed to believe she would—I needed to spend time letting her know me better.

Feeling much as I had the first time Lyssa sent me out to read the wind for money, I plunged into the Hall and found myself swimming through heat. My armpits dampened immediately. Charming. But then from the smell in the room, the fancy folks were sweating too. At the far end of the room, King Thien sat on the platform from which Adrya had led morning prayers. I arrived at the right moment to catch him unbuttoning his collar as he inclined his head to listen to the visiting lord sitting next to him. Adrya sat at Thien's shoulder, a little behind him, her hair, as always, scraped back into a tight knot. It was possible she didn't sweat. With Adrya, who knew?

I searched the folks sitting on the benches. I didn't see Ellyn, but after a moment, I spotted Lineth's smooth dark hair. She was looking straight ahead, face strained, and I saw the bench to either side of her was empty for a good yard. My chest swelled with fury at the stupidity of the folks shunning her. Dodging dancers, I hitched my way along and plunked down next to her.

Her rigid spine loosened a little. "I knew you were someone who kept his promises."

"I could say the same about you, lady." I put the book on the bench between us. When she glanced at it, my face got even hotter. "I thought the refuge kids would like it."

"I'm sure they will. Ellyn told me she likes tales of travel and far away places."

"Good to know." Good enough that I wished I'd known when I was in the library. Judging from the sideways smile Lineth gave me, that thought was written all over my face. I tried to smooth out whatever expression was giving me away and looked at the dancers. At least the dance was familiar. Couples had joined their right hands and were swinging one another around in a country dance I'd seen during festivals in New Square. I scanned the room, trying to look without looking like I was looking. Then, right in front of me, light from the oil lamps glinted off a pale blue gown and a dark dandelion-bloom of curls. My heart lurched. I barely knew Ellyn, and she was suspicious about wind reading. But something of the fierceness implied by the knife that had hung on her belt struck me as just right. A girl needed to be fierce in Rin City.

Then I realized just who was holding her hand and spinning her through the dance. A strand of his lank hair flopped onto his temple as he bent to speak in Ellyn's ear. She flushed and ducked her head, but Dugan turned to me and flashed his teeth in what was more or less a smile. Mostly less.

I felt a savage desire to knock a few of those teeth down Dugan's throat. What's more, a glance at Ellyn's waist told me she wasn't wearing her knife tonight. What was she thinking? If ever there was a place where a girl needed a weapon, a castle dance was it. I entertained myself for a moment with the thought of her gutting Dugan.

Lineth waved to a servant with a tray of wine cups. He approached a little hesitantly. Since I knew he was supposed to serve wine to the nobles and ale to the rest of us, I figured Lineth and I together confused him. Lineth took two cups of wine and passed one to me. "Luckily, we have room for Ellyn to sit with us when this dance is over," she said, matter-of-factly, as if of course Ellyn and I would want to chat. "I don't know Dugan. I take it being roommates hasn't made you friends."

"You take it right." I swallowed a mouthful of wine and had to suppress a grimace. The serving man was right. He shouldn't have wasted Thien's wine on me. Ellyn's back was to me now. I watched from under half-lowered lids as she bent to the steps, graceful as a flower. Ellyn's mouth curved in a faint smile. And really, why shouldn't she smile? Dugan was well-dressed, dripping with admiration and sympathy, and good looking enough if you liked muscles.

After about a year, the music ended, and I sat up straighter, but Dugan kept hold of Ellyn's hand and bent to speak to her. She tipped her ear up to his mouth. My hand tightened on my wine cup. I pulled my crutch in, wondering if I could just leave, but I caught a bit of talk from two men nearby. "Traitor," one of them said, glancing at Lineth. She flushed, and I stayed where I was.

At that moment, a woman in a flame-colored gown appeared at Dugan's side, and I recognized his mother. I took a mean pleasure in how unhappy he looked when Lady Brylla clutched his elbow and steered him to the other side of the room.

All alone, Ellyn turned uncertainly toward the people seated against the wall. I considered waving to her, but Lineth saved me the trouble, and Ellyn hurried toward us. Or rather, hurried toward Lineth, because she hesitated when she saw me. Lineth picked up the book I'd brought and slid away from me to make room, but Ellyn squeezed in on her other side. I beat the tip of my crutch against the floor.

"Jarka brought you this to read to the children," Lineth said.

From the corner of my eye, I saw her offer the book to Ellyn, who took it, and after a moment, leaned forward to see around Lineth. "Thank you. That was kind."

I knew better than to trust a polite word, but that was all it took to make my heart flip over like a runaway cart at the bottom of a hill. "Lady Lineth says you like travel books. I can bring you one if you like."

"I'd appreciate that." Ellyn stroked the cover of the book of tales.

Smiling, Lineth leaned back to give us a better view of one another.

"You want to travel?" I tore my eyes away from Ellyn's caressing hand and forced myself to speak.

"Maybe." She spoke more quickly now. "I want to see what it's like to live in other places. Sometimes folks in Rin fit you in a box and make you live there whether you want to or not."

"Truth enough in that," Lineth murmured.

All three of us sat in silence for a moment. I thought about Clovyan saying I was trying to escape the place I was born to. He was probably right, and plenty of folks would be happy to see me give up and leave the castle. But women and girls got boxed in hard, even a lady like Lineth. Look at Lyssa. Once her first husband died, she tried to earn a living with her needle, but folks paid her only half of what they now paid Clovyan for the same work, even when she still did it.

I glanced across Lineth at Ellyn. "It's not right," I said, and she smiled tentatively.

The musicians struck up a new dance, the courtly kind the nobles liked. "Warn me if Rosin comes this way," Lineth said. It occurred to me that relationship stuff might be complicated for everybody. I wasn't sure if that was comforting or not.

"Is Rosin still bothering you?" I asked.

"He's trying to."

"He's a married man." Ellyn sounded scandalized. I guessed she must not have spent much time in court, where marriages were arranged by parents who spent more time looking at money than anything else. Or in King Thien's case, more at political gain than the treasure his son would have in Lineth. I glanced at the platform where the noble who'd been bending Thien's ear had been replaced by a different one. I shuddered. Poor Beran. Poor Lineth.

I scanned the crowd for Rosin, but my eye caught on a bored looking Dugan sitting next to his mother. As if proving my point, Rosin stood near Brylla, dressed in a shiny pink doublet and clasping the hand of a giggling young woman. He raised the woman's fingers to his lips. Brylla turned away and snapped something at Dugan, who scowled and stomped off to where wine was being served.

"At least you're not the only woman Rosin bothers," I told Lineth, who was watching the same scene.

"He behaved very badly at the refuge," Ellyn said. "Why did he marry her if he's going to flirt with other women right in front of her?"

"She had money?" I suggested.

"Don't be so cynical," Ellyn said. "Maybe he loved her and has just lost his way."

"You just said he behaved badly," I said.

"He did, but that doesn't mean he didn't love her when he married her."

"Now who's cynical? You think real love fails?"

"Sometimes things happen." She frowned and failed to meet my gaze. Unexpectedly, I wondered about her family. My stone mason father fell off a ladder and died before I was born. Lyssa's house was happy enough until Clovyan came along, but I'd not lived very long in a house with a happy marriage to admire. Yet I'd somehow assumed most other people did. Maybe Ellyn had asked for the refuge job because she wanted to get away from home; like traveling, only not. I understood that need.

Dugan returned to his parents with two cups of wine, which his father promptly took, handing one to Brylla and other to the young woman he'd been flirting with. He flicked his fingers to send Dugan back to fetch more. But Brylla had evidently had enough, because she stood and stepped between her husband and the girl. Whatever she said made the girl draw back, curtsy, and scurry away. Rosin caught his wife's arm and snarled something in her ear.

"Maybe she was pregnant." I snorted. "Imagine having Dugan as the reason you married." As soon as I said it, I knew it was a mistake. From clear across Lady Lineth, I saw Ellyn stiffen.

"What's wrong with Dugan?" Ellyn said. "He told me he was urging his parents to donate to the refuge. And if his mother was pregnant, Rosin did the honorable thing."

The wine rippled in Lineth's still full wine cup. Even in the hot room, her face had gone pale. "Dugan shouldn't be judged by his parents."

I immediately felt like a jerk for reminding Lineth of how her father's treason was staining her. I exchanged a guilty look with Ellyn, who quickly said, "You're right, of course."

I watched Dugan return with wine for his father, but

Rosin waved it off, stalked away from his wife, and came straight toward us.

Lineth must have seen him too because she hastily handed her wine to Ellyn and said, "Dance with me, Jarka."

My throat tightened. "I can't." I glanced at Ellyn and then away. This girl moved as fluidly as water. I cringed at the notion of "dancing" in front of her.

Lineth stood. "Please. This dance is easy, I promise."

*It's Lady Lineth*, I reminded myself. I set my wine on the floor, tucked under the bench where no one would kick it over. Then I took a deep breath of sweaty air, rose, and joined her among the dancers. I glimpsed Ellyn smiling, which made me feel lighter.

"For the most part," Lineth said, "all you have to do is stand still. Hold my hand like this." She took my free hand and held it up, which seemed fine until I noticed our left hands were joined, while everyone else held up their rights. I set my jaw and decided it made no difference. In time to the music, she moved away and drew close again. I watched the other men on the floor, who at the moment were standing still, so she'd told the truth when she said this dance was easy, at least so far. Between the other dancers, I saw Rosin frown and turn away.

The next time Lineth drew close, she said, "You're scaring Ellyn off."

The other men all stood on one foot and turned, and I concentrated on pivoting on my crutch. "Because I can read the wind, you mean? If that's it, she scares too easily."

Lineth ducked under my hand, turned, and came to my side with my arm around her shoulders. "Maybe a bit, but sometimes you have an angry air about you that scares a lot of people."

Over Lineth's shoulder, I saw Dugan swagger into sight and sit next to Ellyn. He picked up the book of tales, listened to something she said, and laughed.

"Ouch," Lineth said.

Hastily, I loosened my grip on her fingers. "Sorry." I saw Ellyn snatch the book back from Dugan before Lineth turned us around, and I couldn't see them anymore. *Take that, Dugan.*

When Lineth came near again, I said, "I have no idea what you mean. Do I scare *you*?"

Without answering, she halted right in the middle of the dance floor, one hand on her chest. When I looked more closely, I saw her pale face was tinged faintly green.

"Are you all right?" I asked.

"I don't think I am."

Someone in a flame-red gown stopped next to us, enveloping me in a cloud of musk and sweat, and I turned to see Lady Brylla, clutching the arm of a sullen looking Dugan. Rosin was nowhere in sight. Judging by the look on his wife's face, I assumed he'd slipped away with that pretty girl. Call me cynical.

Brylla looked me up and down, her lip curling, then yanked Dugan forward. "Ask Lady Lineth to dance,

Dugan. I'm sure she'd appreciate a partner with some polish."

Dugan took a step toward Lineth, but she was already curtsying. "I'm sorry, but I'm not feeling well and was just telling Jarka I needed to leave. Fair night, Jarka. Thank you for coming." She slipped between the dancers and disappeared.

"You missed your chance," Brylla snapped at her son. "Next time do as you're told."

"Sorry," he muttered, shooting me a murderous look, as if I meant to be there listening to them be nasty to one another.

"Come," Brylla said. Ignoring me as if I weren't worth wasting eyesight on, she sailed from the Hall with Dugan at her heels like a pet dog.

All right then. The keeping-Lineth-company part of the evening was over, so I was free to leave. I glanced over at Ellyn. For an instant, I thought she was looking at me, but her gaze slid away to the musicians in the gallery over my head, though at the moment they weren't playing. An empty space yawned next to her where Dugan had sat. If I left, maybe she'd feel lonely and awkward. Dancers were moving onto the floor again, and a man went out of his way to jostle me, making it clear I was in the way. Why was I hesitating? It wasn't like Ellyn was carrying her knife. Besides, it would be rude to leave without saying farewell.

Trying to smother any "angry" air I might be giving

off, I headed her way. Her eyes dropped from the gallery just as my foot connected with my cup under the bench and wine flooded under the soles of her shoes. "Move!" I barked. With a cry, she jumped to her feet so fast that more wine slopped out of Lady Lineth's cup still clutched in her hand. With a moan, she set the nearly empty cup on the bench, grabbed the book of tales, and joined me in scrambling along the edge of the room until we found space for two. We sat, both leaning back so people to either side of us hid us.

"Should we have cleaned that up?" she asked, breathless from hurry.

"We'd deprive some castle worker of a job if we did." Our gazes met and simultaneously we laughed. "Only one good foot and I kick over my wine," I said ruefully.

She peeled one wine stained slipper from the floor with a tiny sucking noise. "I hope Lady Lineth doesn't want that cup back."

"She left. She said she wasn't feeling well, but I think she may have been trying to escape—" I stopped myself in time from saying something that might sound critical of Dugan. "—the close air in here," I finished.

"You were kind to dance with her."

I struggled for breath. "She's easy to be kind to."

"She speaks highly of you."

I caught myself smiling. For a few moments, we sat in silence, watching the dancers. When she put the book on the bench between us, her fingertips brushed my thigh, making me jump. She jerked her hand away and flushed. I definitely looked not-angry, which seemed to be doing the trick. The musicians launched into a new tune, and the folks on either side of us got up to dance. I watched to see how difficult the dance was. Maybe Ellyn wouldn't mind if I asked her to join it. I wiped sweaty palms on my trousers.

"Wyswoman Adrya is beckoning to you," she said.

"The Powers save me," I turned my face away from the platform which had the merit of being toward Ellyn. "Pretend you don't see."

"Do you usually sit with her and the king at dances?"

"This is the first time I've been to one, so I don't *usually* do anything. She probably wants to lecture me, fill me with Wys knowledge."

"What's wrong with Wys knowledge?"

"Nothing. I want as much as I can get. I just don't want to sit with Adrya at a dance." *I'd rather sit with you,* I did not add.

She crossed her arms in her lap. "Are you planning to give up wind reading to become a Wysman?"

"Of course not. Beran only chose me for that. Why else would he have picked a street kid with one good leg? I can use wind reading and Adrya's wisdom too."

"For what?" Her drawn brows turned into a full-blown frown. I frowned back. I'd done nothing to earn the suspicion in her voice.

"To be an adviser for Thien and eventually Beran so they can be good kings."

"I think Thien is already a good king, and his Wyswoman relies only on human learning. He let Lady Lineth use some of her fortune for the refuge."

"He didn't know she was doing that until today and he questioned it," I heard myself say. "As far as I can see, he spends exactly no time thinking about folks like street kids. Also, notice he won't let Prince Beran marry Lineth because he wants to use Beran's marriage to seal a bargain with a lord somewhere else. If Thien puts the peace of Rinland above his own son's happiness, what do you think he would do for Rena and Laren?"

"A good king is supposed to put the country's wellbeing ahead of his own family's. And I don't see why you need sorcery to give good advice." She turned to face me and her voice grew tenser.

"You insult a gift of the Powers when you use a word like 'sorcery.' Wind reading is just a way to channel one of the elements and let the Powers speak through it. What I mean to do is make sure Thien knows what the common people need."

"You mean force it into his mind." Her whole body went rigid. "You have no right to that kind of power. No one does. I was ensorcelled once and my little brother died because I wasn't able to watch him."

"What?"

"I was ensorcelled." She picked up the book and pressed it to her stomach. "I don't know who did it or how, but I was." She turned her head stiffly toward me.

"You're the first wind reader I've talked to, and I thought maybe you would explain what happened, but you don't believe me, do you?"

"It's not that I don't believe you—"

"I can see you don't. That's all right. My parents didn't either." She jumped to her feet and strode away, skirts swinging, leaving two smudged wine-colored footprints as the only sign she'd been there.

I rubbed my hand over my face. That was strange. Could anyone ensorcell someone else? I had a sudden flash of sympathy for the guard on the walkway that morning. I felt about Ellyn's claim the same way he'd apparently felt about mine. My only comfort was she took the book. The next time I saw Lady Lineth, I would point out I hadn't been the only one here with an angry air.

When a serving man stopped in front of me, I shook my head at more wine, but he said, "Wyswoman Adrya wants you," and walked away without offering me any. Suppressing a sigh, I rose and went towards the platform, skirting the sticky wine spill.

When I got there, Adrya pointed at a stool. "Get that and sit here," she ordered. Now there was a woman who was *not* shut in a box. I pulled it up next to her and lowered myself carefully. She leaned close enough for me to smell her rose perfume. "Watch and listen to His Majesty as he deals with his lords. Ruling also happens in places other than the council chamber."

She was undoubtedly right, but she was between me

and Thien, and the music was loud, and I couldn't hear the king, much less the noble whispering to him. I wondered how long I had to stay.

A taste like wild mushrooms slipped onto my tongue just as the barest of breezes blew over my face. Puzzled, I looked up at the high windows. The banners hanging from the rafters rippled and then curled sideways. At the same moment, the torches flared, and the floor shivered. Heart pounding, I shoved to my feet.

Near the doors into the antechamber, someone squealed, "water!" The crowd swirled noisily, some people pushing out the doors and others backing away from what I now saw was water flooding into the Hall. Tower Guards who'd been discreetly stationed against the walls rushed forward to surround Thien and hustle him, protesting, out through the door at the back of the platform.

"Elemental power," I croaked at Adrya. "And it's gone wrong."

# Chapter 6

A DRYA SHOT ME one disbelieving look before she gathered her skirts, stepped down from the platform, and strode toward the Hall entrance with me hitching after her. We joined a crowd wading through an inch-deep pool in the antechamber. The flood was coming from the courtyard, and when we emerged into it, I saw water shooting from the fountain ten feet up into the torch-lit night sky. The courtyard was ankle deep in icy water. I staggered under the press of the churned up and battering elements. I could see the pulse of Adrya's blood on the side of her neck. She gripped her Wyswoman pendant and moved her lips in a prayer I couldn't hear over people crying out in shock when they waded into a flood on what should be dry stone. They might not know it was mishandled power they felt, but they knew their world was atilt and they knew enough to be afraid.

The jet of water roared a yard higher. The woman on

Adrya's right screamed. At the front of the crowd, folks were starting to back up, making people behind them shout about being stepped on and shoved.

"Can you do something?" Adrya asked, startling me.

"No, but look."

She turned from me to the fountain. "Look," she echoed in the voice that carried to every corner of the Hall every morning. "The flow is easing." Sure enough, it was. The spout of water was dropping so much so that within a few heartbeats, it collapsed back into the basin. "Someone probably broke a pipe when preparing to put up the Darklight wheel. Nothing to worry about."

For a moment, the crowd teetered on the edge of panic. Then someone up front said, "The level in the basin is falling." He gave a laugh that was shaky but reassuring. The woman next to Adrya swallowed her scream. I could feel the relief spreading through the yard. The world was as they'd always believed it to be after all.

"It's rotten use of water, Adrya," I told her under my breath. "I'll get my wind box and see what it tells us."

"No." She drew me out of the way of people drifting back into the castle, shaking wet shoes and skirt hems. "The idea of something unnatural was what frightened people. The sight of a wind box will set them into a panic and start trouble His Majesty neither needs nor wants. Something has simply broken in the fountain."

"But—"

"No, Jarka. I forbid it. The party is breaking up with

the Hall flooded. Go to bed. I'll see you in the morning."

Sloshing through an inch of water, I followed everyone else. I'd never tried to read the wind with the elements all churned up like this. Any reading would be hard to make out. But Adrya was wrong. The power I felt was an ancient force, rooted in earth, wind, fire, and water. This was channeling done badly so the wild part of water had broken free. This was danger we pretended was gone, coming to call. The face of the dead boy flickered behind my eyes and then faded. That warning was done, worn out. I'd missed whatever it had to tell me. We'd have to see what happened next.

I SNAPPED AWAKE, jerking halfway up, heart pounding. Close by, someone let out a bone-rattling snore. I blinked at the whitewashed wall, then flopped back onto my bed. Not Lyssa's house or some rat-infested bolt hole: I was in my bed in the boys' dormitory, listening to someone snore in the next room. I swiped a corner of the sheet over my sweaty face and neck. I'd dreamed of Clovyan beating me again. Unwilling to close my eyes and chance falling back to sleep and Clovyan, I stared across the room at the runes on the wall at the foot of Dugan's empty bed. Something *thwapped* the wall of the next room. The snorer inhaled wildly and, after a moment, the two boys who lived there shared a laugh. I sighed.

My bad foot ached. I massaged it and tried to figure out how to track down whoever had set crooked power working last night. A breeze snuck under the bottom edge of the leather curtain, ruffled a nightshirt Dugan had thrown under the washstand, and swirled to caress my face. *You dunce*, I thought in disgust. *Ever hear of reading the wind?* My only excuse was I was sleepy and distracted by thoughts of Clovyan. This early, other folks wouldn't be up to see me read the wind and take fright. The room was chilly enough that I washed and dressed in a hurry. Dugan had been whining for days now that the dormitory master should let us keep the brazier we'd had in the room all winter. I huffed but couldn't see my breath. Dugan should try sleeping in an alley.

Shouldering my bag, I slipped out of the room and limped through the twisting castle hallways and out to the sharp-aired dawn. I picked my way across dew-slicked stones still dotted with puddles from the night before. I was passing through the gate to the old keep when something froze me in place, my body halting before I realized what had stopped me. Close by, a woman had given a strangled cry. In the dark corner next to the stairs leading up to the wall, a curly-haired woman in a blue gown bent over something I couldn't see. In an eyeblink, I recognized Ellyn. She must have heard me thumping toward her because she sprang to her feet and spun to face me, her knife in her hand, standing guard over the small figure on the ground. I drew a sharp breath and flung myself awkwardly to my knees. Rena sprawled on the stones like a heap of rags, bruises circling her wrists like blue bracelets. The stones under her were dark with moisture. Her gown was wet. She smelled very faintly of something sweet.

I thrust my hand a finger's width from her nose and open mouth, then held my breath as I waited for hers. What seeped out of her instead felt like cold mist. I rested my shaking hand on her shoulder, and something simultaneously familiar and strange shivered under my palm. She tingled with power, but power so twisted it sent a sick chill into my chest.

"What happened?" I asked.

"I don't know! She was missing when I went back to the refuge last night."

A man in rumpled satin strolled through the gate from the main yard—Rosin, still in the embroidered pink doublet he'd worn at the previous night's dancing. It dawned on me that Ellyn too wore the clothes she'd had on the previous night. She must not have been to bed at all. Rosin took one look at Rena and did what Ellyn and I should have done. "Help!" he shouted. "Help!"

Footsteps thundered down the stairs. The young guard I'd seen the previous morning jumped down the last three steps and swung toward us, sword in hand. "What is it?"

"I just arrived." Rosin pointed shakily at Rena and then at me and Ellyn. "I came through the gate and there they were."

"Drop the knife," the guard ordered Ellyn. She started to resheathe it, but the guard said, "No. Drop it on the ground." Looking confused, Ellyn let it fall to the flagstones. She was obviously less used to being ordered around by guards or watchmen than I was. The guard focused on Rena, then swept his gaze over my bag, and stared wide-eyed into my face. "I knew I should have arrested you. What did you do to her?" He centered the point of his sword on my breast.

"Nothing!" I said. "We found her like this, right, Ellyn? She needs the infirmary." I cursed the crutch that kept me from carrying her there.

"Tell me the way, and I'll take her." Ellyn crouched and slid her arms under Rena.

"No." The guard waved the tip of his sword toward Rosin. "You take her." Rosin held up his hands as if touching Rena might hurt. "Do it!" the guard said. With a groan, Rosin scooped Rena into his arms and hurried inside. Ellyn started after him but the guard barked, "You stay here. How did you get into the castle grounds?"

"The gate guard let me in to search for her." Ellyn gestured after Rena. "She's from the refuge. I'm supposed to be looking after her."

Was I mistaken that a note of bitterness overlaid the words "supposed to be"?

"You found her with him?" the guard asked, moving both himself and his pointy sword tip closer to me.

To my great relief, Ellyn said, "No. I got here first."

"We didn't do anything," I said. "This is connected to what happened with the fountain last night. That kid is full of badly used elemental energy."

"You call up sorcery every morning," the guard said. "I've seen you." From the corner of my eye, I glimpsed Ellyn biting her lip. The guard shifted from foot to foot. "Get out of the castle," he finally told Ellyn.

"Not until I see to Rena," she said. "I'm responsible, and she'll be scared if she wakes up all alone. She probably came in here last night looking for me."

"Suit yourself," the guard said. "Move." He waved us toward the old tower.

"You can't mean to put us in a cell," I said. Even when I lived on the streets, I'd never landed in a cell. The idea of being locked up at the mercy of this guard or anyone else made my breath come fast and shallow. "Someone hurt that little girl, and we need to find out who."

"That assumes we don't already know." The guard dipped to pick up Ellyn's knife. Her eyes followed it anxiously. "Move," the guard repeated.

We walked ahead of him to the keep's thick wooden door. When the door opened, he waved us through ahead of him into what turned out to be a stone corridor with doors on either side and the jailer holding the door open. "Prisoners for you," our guard said. I scarcely heard him over my heart pounding in my ears.

"All right if I put them together? We're full up with

drunken stable hands who staged a brawl just before dawn." The jailer took a ring of keys from a hook on the wall, unlocked the door closest to him, and opened it into a dimly lit cell.

I swallowed hard. Clovyan had trapped me in the small storeroom at the back of his house. His fists had driven into my face, my ribs, my gut.

"How long will we be here?" Ellyn asked from far away. "Rena needs me, and there's a house full of children and another minder depending on me."

"You had your chance to leave," our guard said. "Get in there." He reached for my bag, but at the last moment, curled his fingers back as if it might burn him.

My vision blurred. I took Ellyn's arm and pretended I wasn't leaning on her as I urged her forward. The jailer shut the door behind us, and the key snicked in the lock.

"I'll be back as soon as I'm off duty," our guard said. "I want to talk to them."

"You going to report to the captain, Gelas?" The jailer sounded skeptical.

"Eventually," our guard, Gelas?, said.

I called, "Send for Wyswoman Adrya. She'll straighten this out." The only answer was the thump of boots walking away followed by the thud of the door. I grabbed at the thought that I was missing prayers. Adrya would know something was wrong. A drop of sweat tickled down my neck.

Pink dawn light slanted along the ceiling from small

openings over our heads. There were benches along either wall, probably meant to serve as beds, though they'd be mighty uncomfortable for sleeping. Not an accident, I supposed. I lowered myself onto one and set my bag beside me with a hand that shook only a little.

"What happened?" I asked.

Ellyn collapsed next to me, close enough that our shoulders brushed. She didn't move away, so maybe, like me, she needed the comfort of shared warmth. There were circles under her eyes and her gown was crumpled and grey with dirt where she'd knelt in the yard. "I told you I don't know."

"You said she was gone when you went home last night." I tried to shut Gelas—and Clovyan—out of my head. I needed to think clearly. Whoever hurt Rena tried to use elemental power to do it, and I was the only one likely to have a clue about how that happened. "You left the dancing pretty early. Where was Tally when Rena vanished?"

Ellyn looked away. "I didn't go straight home. Lady Lineth said I didn't have to, and I was glad of the break. I should have been there. I should have been keeping watch." Her hands twisted together in her lap as if she were trying to keep something—or someone—from slipping away.

I slapped at what felt like a spider web against my ear, but it turned out to be a strand of my own hair, drifting in the cool air that fell from the openings overhead. Sweet

Powers, I was jumpy. *Clovyan isn't here, Braveheart*, I told myself. *That guard is coming back though*, answered a nasty voice in the back of my head. "So how long was it before you went to the refuge?"

"I'm not sure."

An image of her and Dugan dancing popped into my head. He'd left early too, and Ellyn had been angry at me and sympathetic to him. "Where did you go?" The question came out rougher than I meant it to, and she flinched.

"Just to the courtyard. You can hear the music from there."

*You could even dance to it.* "And then?"

"I went to the refuge, and I thought everyone was asleep, but when I passed Rena's bed, I saw it was empty. So I woke up Tally, but she said Rena was there when she went to bed."

"She wasn't in her nightgown," I said. "She must have gotten up and dressed."

In the next cell, someone groaned, then retched. Chunky liquid spattered on the floor.

"She would have been dressed anyway," Ellyn said. "The kids were upset that Lineth and I were both gone. You know how it is. Some of them have been abandoned. Tally couldn't manage them, and a few went to bed in their clothes, including Rena."

"Why didn't you come and get me?" It came out like an accusation. I couldn't believe she let her anger at me get in the way of looking for a lost kid.

She frowned at me. "I did go back to the Hall, but you were sitting with the king, and obviously I could search the courtyard myself. Folks were still going in and out through the gate. She could easily have come in trying to find me."

Our gazes met, and I knew we both saw the same big hole in that explanation. "Would she have left Laren?"

"Never!" She sounded close to tears. "I should have admitted it right away, but finally I got scared enough to ask one of the gate guards for help. He asked if she'd ever run away before, and I had to admit she did just that morning. He didn't understand about Laren. And then the fountain erupted." Her eyes went wide and her hands tightened into fists. She glanced at me, then away.

"It scared me too," I said and cautiously put my arm around her shoulders.

She met my gaze for a long moment, seemed to judge what she saw, and leaned against me. The smell of vomit drifted through the barred window in the door of our cell. It occurred to me that any other setting would have been more romantic. "After that the guards had no time for me," Ellyn said. "All I could think to do was go down to New Square, asking folks along the way if they'd seen her."

"By yourself at night? Do you know how dangerous that is?"

"I think I have an idea," she said more sharply than I expected. "You're not the only one with sense, Jarka."

"Sorry," I forced out. "I didn't mean that the way it

sounded." I had to fight for breath when I thought of things that happened to girls I knew on the streets. Boys, too, if they were alone. I shoved the memory into the dark hole where it usually lived. Wisps of hair tickled my forehead again. I snapped my spine straight. I was the world's slowest fool. My only excuse was that I was scared stupid, for Rena and, in the back of my head where I couldn't drag it out, for me too. Also, I'd been hugging Ellyn and now I had to let her go. I pulled my wind box out of my bag and yanked on the string that tugged it into shape.

"What are you doing?" Ellyn leaned away.

"Finding out what's going on." I held the bag of paper bits out to her. Sliding farther off, she shook her head. "It's not going to hurt you!" I said. "Come on! We need to know." She shook her head again. "All right. I'll do it myself. I'm the one who missed all the warnings so it should be me anyway."

I dumped the paper into my hand and spoke the invocation as I flung it into the box. Ellyn cringed as if she thought the box would catch fire. That splashed cold water on my fantasy life. *This is what I am*, I thought fiercely. *This is my only gift and I'm using it. If you don't like it, too bad. You won't be the first. Clovyan hated it enough he tried to beat it out of me.* I asked, "Where is this broken power coming from?" and blew on the paper bits. They stirred, but for a moment, didn't move, as if the wind was annoyed at me for ignoring the way it had been calling me since I first woke up. Then wind swirled into the box and the paper danced.

I concentrated on the drift of confetti, stirred by my breath and the finger of wind that had finally answered me. A rush of emotions swept over me. I was a little girl, hurtling into the day, eager for what she'd find. And what she saw was me—Jarka—coming out the castle gate, then a flash in which the gate shrank to a narrow hole, then me and the gate, then the hole, alternating like the figures on a Darklight wheel. I caught a fleeting whiff of something flowery but with a sharp edge. My mouth flooded with the minty taste of horehound.

Before I had time to scrabble up the barest understanding of what any of that meant, I heard the keep door open and close, and Gelas, the young guard from the walkway, said, "You can take a break. I'll watch them."

# Chapter 7

"THE PLACE IS all yours," the jailer said. "The mop's in the cupboard at the end of the hall. You'll need it."

All the air seemed to have been sucked out of our cell. The door had barely slammed behind the jailer before the key turned in our lock and Gelas loomed in the doorway. His eyes went straight to the wind box. "Stone you," he cursed. As if Ellyn or I or maybe the box might jump him, he drew his sword.

"What are you doing?" Ellyn sprang to her feet.

I yanked the string to collapse the box and stuffed it out of sight in my carry bag, paper bits spitting all around. "It's not going to hurt you," I babbled around the clog in my throat.

He breathed hard enough to shiver the thin hair of his moustache. "You're either a liar or a fool. Everyone in here is in danger as long as that filth is in the castle. Look at what happened to the fountain." He snorted, making his moustache quiver again. "They said a pipe broke. Not likely."

He was perceptive. I'd give him that. I wondered if, without knowing it, he had a feeling for the elements, like I did. That could be scaring him stupid.

Ellyn took a step toward him. "It's all right," she said in the voice she probably used on panicked street kids. "Jarka put the box away. He's not using it now. We're safe."

I tied the thong holding the bag shut. "There. See? All gone."

His eyes darted side to side. When he spoke, his voice was soft enough he might have been talking to himself. "My old auntie used to say sorcery lived in the blood. I shouldn't be fooled. The things a sorcerer uses are just tricks." His gaze steadied on me, pinning me like a paper target on a board in the guards' training yard.

I swallowed hard. He was between me and the door. For a moment, he faded away and Clovyan appeared. I shook my head to clear my vision, and a drop of sweat flew off.

Gelas slid his sword back into its sheath. I sagged with relief. He was going to be reasonable after all. Then he pulled a knife from his belt and stepped toward me. "It's the right thing to do." He nodded in agreement with himself. "I'll just make a tiny prick. It won't kill you, just clean you."

A blur moved at the edge of my vision, and Ellyn lunged between us. "That's my knife," she said crisply. "Give it to me, please." She held out her hand as if she expected to be obeyed. I thought again that she must have never once come under a watchman's suspicious gaze.

"Out of the way." He shoved her just as she reached for the knife, and the blade sliced across her arm. She cried out and clapped her other hand over the cut.

I launched myself at the guard, caught him around the waist, and toppled him flat. The knife clattered out of his grip and spun across the floor. I'd been in street fights, but Gelas was a trained soldier who was bigger than me and had two good feet. If I didn't knock him out now, he'd take his chance to bleed all the "sorcery" out of me. I punched him in the neck.

Ellyn screamed, "Stop! Stop!"

The guard heaved me off him. I fell back and was only vaguely aware of the cell door moving out of the way of my skull.

"What is going on in here?" a woman demanded. Gelas lifted his head, and I rolled my eyes upward to see Adrya standing in the doorway. "Get off him," she ordered.

A little to my surprise, the guard did.

I dragged myself toward my crutch. Ellyn grabbed it and held it out to me. Blood dripped from her arm. Guilt choked me, followed closely by humiliation that she'd had to defend me.

"Why did no one tell me my apprentice was being held?" Adrya demanded of the guard. Gelas climbed to his feet and stood rubbing the side of his neck I'd slugged.

"He's Tower Guard business," he muttered. "Not yours."

"I disagree," she snapped. "And you have things to do. Your other prisoners need attention." She stepped out of the doorway, clearing it for him. Adrya was tall for a woman, and she tilted her head back so she could look down her nose at him. He shuffled his feet but backed out of the cell and looked down the hallway toward where someone was vomiting hard enough that his teeth probably landed in the puddle. Adrya jerked her head in that direction. Gelas grimaced, then moved toward the end of the hallway where the jailer said the mop was kept.

"There's something wrong with him," Ellyn whispered.

There was. He was much less in control of his fear than he'd been the previous morning. I wondered uneasily if the broken power had slid inside his head.

Adrya looked pointedly around the cell and raised an eyebrow. "What did you do to merit this?"

"*We* didn't do anything. Someone tried to use water's energy on a kid," I said. "Like with the fountain, it went wrong."

"I heard a child was hurt." Adrya pulled Ellyn's arm straight and examined the cut. She took a clean handkerchief from her pocket and pressed it against the wound. "Go to the infirmary and have them look at this. It appears to be shallow but it's best to be careful. The little girl is still there if you want to check on her. Ask a door guard to show you the way. Tell him I said it was allowed." She dropped Ellyn's arm and stepped away, gesturing toward the door.

Ellyn took the time to pick up her knife and wipe her own blood from it onto Adrya's handkerchief before sliding it into its sheath. "Jarka didn't do anything to Rena. The guard was unfair."

I snorted at the word "unfair," thinking for the third time that she'd obviously never been a street kid. Still, given how she'd reacted to the wind box, that must have been hard for her to say. Something warm sparked in my chest.

"I'll go with you," I said. "The healer won't know what he's looking at in Rena."

"You stay," Adrya said. "I need to talk to you."

Ellyn turned to me and hesitated. "I'll come later," I said. She gave me a nod and left the cell. I watched her go, the spark of happiness still alive. I heard the keep door *thunk* behind her before Adrya closed the one to the cell, shutting us in. The spark went out. *The door's unlocked*, I reminded myself. *I can leave.*

Farther down the hall, Gelas snarled, "Here. Mop up after yourself."

Adrya sat where Ellyn had been. "What do you know about the girl?"

I moved to the door and peeked through the bars, trying to see where Gelas was. "Her name is Rena. I don't know anything about her other than I found her and her little brother near the South Gate."

"Not her," Adrya said dismissively enough to annoy me. "The refuge mistress. You sat with her last night, I noticed. Is she related to the cutler with the shop just off the South Market?"

I turned to look at her. In the dim light, her face was half in shadows. "I don't know. Her name is Ellyn. Lady Lineth hired her."

Adrya clutched the Wyswoman pendant she wore, the one shaped like *The Book of the Wys*. "That was a very fine knife," she murmured, face vague enough that her mind was obviously far away. "Her father could have made it."

I pictured a father who'd had one child killed making a weapon for his daughter. "She's not afraid to wave it around either, which is a good thing given the attack on Rena." I was unable to suppress a smile.

Adrya dragged herself back and narrowed her eyes. "Rosin came to see me. How was he involved in what happened this morning?"

"He stumbled across Ellyn and me standing over Rena and started yelling for help."

"He wasn't with the girl, then?"

"No." I tried to remember exactly what Rosin had done. "He looked like he'd been out all night. And he didn't want to touch Rena. The guard made him."

Adrya glanced at the closed cell door and lowered her voice. "I'm going to tell you something that you must keep to yourself. If you can't do that, you'll have to stay in this cell until Lord Rosin and Lady Brylla leave for home."

"What?" The walls inched inward. "Why?"

"You've alarmed Rosin. He's an old friend, so he came to see me and complain about you. You know from attending council meetings that His Majesty is wary of another rebellion in Lac's Holding, and Rosin controls the only bridge they could use to come north. I need to be sure you won't pursue Rosin over this matter."

"I blocked him from dancing with Lady Lineth last night but haven't gone after him at all, much less about the fountain or Rena."

"He's afraid you will."

"Why?" A memory flickered to life. "Yesterday morning, after prayers, Thien asked about something Rosin's uncle did. What was that about?"

She shifted on the bench. "Sit so I can keep my voice down."

I peeled myself off the cell door and dropped to the bench opposite her.

"I say again this must go no farther, not even, or really especially, to that girl, no matter how pretty she is."

In the hall, Gelas shouted, "If you're beat up, it's your own fault."

"I'm not staying in this cell," I said.

"Very well." She drew a deep breath. "You've

undoubtedly noticed that Rosin looks young for his age."

"I don't know his age. He does look young."

"As it happens, he's three years older than I am."

"Not possible," I blurted before realizing it was rude.

"I've known him a long time." She cocked her head and smiled at some memory. "Nine years ago, Rosin's uncle tried to channel elemental power. There's a history of channelers in that family."

"Brylla said something like that when she came to visit the refuge. She thought Dugan should be your apprentice."

"The uncle found a way to use water's power to give youth back to Rosin."

My breath stopped. In my head, the tale of the Grabber bumped up against *The Book of the Wys* passage Adrya had aimed straight at Rosin. *Our divine parents care for us as we care for our own children. To harm them for our own desires would be an abomination.* "The uncle took it from a child."

Adrya nodded. "He did. It worked, but the uncle was executed because the little boy died." She watched me as if waiting for me to make a connection.

A boy killed by elemental power, I thought, and the answer snapped into place. "Ellyn's little brother."

"Yes."

My brain raced. "Water, you say? Rosin must be trying it on his own. He tried to use Rena, and that's why the fountain went wild."

"I know the man," she said, a note I didn't recognize in her voice. "He's frivolous and vain and selfish, but he wouldn't do what his uncle did. He's not brave enough. Besides, you said yourself he wasn't there."

"But before we found her—"

"No. He promised Thien and me too that he'd never touch elemental power again. What's more, he doesn't know how, and he doesn't have access to the tools to learn. I saw to that."

"If his uncle could find out, so could he."

"No, Jarka. When he came to me this morning, he was frightened he might be blamed. Thien had warned him that if he broke his promise, his life was forfeit. And then, when Dugan was old enough to be a squire, Thien brought him to the castle as a hostage against bad behavior."

'Bad behavior' was a weak term for stealing a child's life. "So Rosin gets away with the benefit of a child's murder because Thien needs him to guard the bridge."

"Rosin didn't know what the uncle planned."

"I don't know how this channeling worked, and I'm guessing you're not going to tell me," I said. "But Rosin must have seen his uncle drag a kid into wherever they were. Didn't that strike him as wrong?"

"He said everything happened too fast." She caressed her pendant. "And he didn't get away entirely unpunished. He paid a large fine to Ellyn's family."

"A fine," I said flatly.

She flicked her gaze away from me. "Poor people need money."

"That shop does good business." I waited to see if she had more excuses, but she kept silent. "Does Ellyn know Rosin was involved in her brother's death?"

"I don't believe so. Keeping quiet was one of the conditions for getting the payment."

So that was why Ellyn's parents hadn't believed her about being 'ensorcelled.' Or that was why they said they didn't. My sympathy for her father's arming her blew away. Did he think a knife made up for making her shoulder a blame that wasn't hers? No wonder she talked about what was or wasn't fair. Even if she didn't know the truth, she must sense something awry.

Adrya dropped the pendant. "So I need a pledge from you, Jarka. You'll stay away from Rosin, which you should be willing to promise because he's unlikely to have had anything to do with this child, Rena. I'm not sure anyone did. You're the only one who blames her condition on elemental power."

I snapped my sagging jaw shut. "Then what do you think happened to her?"

"Children get sick." She shrugged.

Fury made me grip the strap of my bag so hard that it cut into my palm. "Is this how Wyswomen and Wysmen wind up thinking if they serve a king?"

"Rulers make hard choices," she said. "Everyone does. If you never have to, count yourself lucky."

"I'm making one of those choices right now." I heaved a deep breath. "Very well," I forced out, "I'll stay away from him." That didn't mean I wouldn't learn whatever

Rosin had done, though. Bad power had been used on a child, and Rosin had been involved in it before. I'd ask around about where he'd spent the night as soon as I'd checked on Rena and Ellyn. The thought of the cut on Ellyn's arm made me cringe. What kind of man let a woman dodge between him and a knife?

I rose and took a step toward the cell door, but Adrya stayed where she was as if she had more to say. I felt a stab of apprehension. "I also need to keep your wind box until Rosin is gone."

"No." I backed as far from her as I could get in the tiny cell.

"It's only for a few days. Rosin says he's afraid you'll use it as an excuse to lie about him."

"Prince Beran gave me this box. My wind reading is why I'm in the castle. It's what he values in me."

"I understand, but once again, if you can't do as you're asked, you'll have to stay here until Rosin leaves."

Right through the bag, I felt the box throb against my hip. But I had no time to waste. Darklight was in three days. After that, Rosin would go home, and I'd lose my chance to prove he'd abused a child. I slid the bag from my shoulder and held it out. Adrya took it, and I felt as if she'd ripped part of the world out of my grip.

"Thank you. I'll keep it safe." She opened the cell door, and I followed her into the hallway. Gelas was there with a mop and bucket. His gaze bored into my back until I was out in the yard with the door shut behind me.

# Chapter 8

B LINKING IN THE late morning light, I followed Adrya through the gate to the main courtyard and found that while I'd been locked in a cell, preparations for the Darklight celebration had gone on. Men stood in and around the fountain putting up the Darklight wheel. Kitchen staff had set up tables and were loading them with bread, fruit, and pastries. Visitors and workers from the sprawling castle household milled about, grabbing a quick handful of food or offering advice to the men in the fountain.

I'd not eaten yet, and my stomach was remembering street life and getting ready to panic, but I hovered next to Adrya, burning to snatch my carry bag back. She stopped and tapped the stable master's shoulder and when he turned, she suggested he check on his arrested men.

Rosin wasn't in the yard, which was a good thing, because despite what I promised Adrya I might not have been able to stop myself from pinning him to a wall and asking him what he'd done to Rena. Adrya might say he didn't know how to channel water's power, but he'd been there when his uncle did. He *had* to have learned something from that.

As the stable master strode toward the old keep, a guard munching on a nut roll came hustling toward me. "Did you see the messenger from your cousin?" he asked. "I sent him into the Hall during prayers, but he said he couldn't find you."

My heart sped up. "Do you know what was in the message?"

The guard wiped honey from his chin. "She wants you to come and see her right away. You're to bring your wind box." He wrinkled his nose, then trotted back toward his post at the gate.

I whirled toward Adrya who'd plainly heard because she pressed my bag tightly against her side. "Go ahead. Spend your holiday as you like."

"I need my box."

"No."

I opened and closed my hand, feeling how right it would be to snatch the carry bag from her shoulder.

"This is for your own good, Jarka."

I'd heard that one before. I wiped my empty hand over my face. If Lyssa had paid a messenger and asked for the wind box, something had shaken her. I had to get to her place right now. "Adrya, can you see how Rena and Ellyn are? See if they need any help."

She patted my arm, but I jerked out of her reach. "The healer will give them good care. You don't need to worry. Go see your cousin."

I headed toward the gate, stopping only to snatch up two pastries. Crowds of holiday shoppers mobbed Kings Way, and I veered off onto a side street as soon as I could. What could Lyssa want? She needed to listen to me and leave Clovyan. She and Izzy were in as much danger as Rena had been when she ran into Rosin. At that thought, a question popped into my head but before I could go after it, I set my crutch wrong, slipped, and had to fight to stay upright, dropping one of the pastries. I paused for a moment, making sure I was back in control of my body. I felt unbalanced without my wind box on my shoulder.

I started toward Lyssa's again, mulling over possible answers to what I should have asked sooner. How had Rena met her attacker? When Tally last saw her, she was in her bed next to Laren's. Had Rosin somehow got into the refuge? The door had a good strong lock. I'd made sure of that when I found the house for Lady Lineth.

Right in front of me, a woman came out of a house, a marketing basket over her arm. She pulled her door shut, locked it, and tucked the key in her pocket. At the sight of her, a further question nearly sent me staggering again. Ellyn had been out when Rena vanished. Surely she knew better than to leave the refuge door unlocked.

I rounded the corner onto Lyssa's street, and the

tension in my shoulders eased when I saw her leaning on the counter at the window, idly watching passers-by. She looked unbruised from where I stood. I whistled softly. She glanced my way, then jerked back out of sight and a moment later slipped out the door, shutting it softly behind her. She grabbed my arm, the muscles of her jaw tight. Clovyan must be in the shop.

"Let's go around the corner." She led me toward the shelter of a narrow lane where the householder next door had built a chicken coop. The hens flapped and scolded, then settled down, muttering to themselves. "It's good to see you." She stretched to kiss my cheek. "One of the neighbors said you were here yesterday. Is something the matter?"

"You sent for me to ask me that?"

"I didn't send for you."

"But I got a message. I thought maybe Clovyan—"

"Hush." Her mouth pinched. "I've told you before I won't listen to any talk against him. Me and Izzy need to eat."

I picked up the tip of my crutch and banged it down again. "If you leave him, I can help you. I'll find someplace for you to go, and sometimes I read the wind for castle folks and earn coin I can give you." I dug out the packet of smashed horehound drops still in my pocket and put it in her hand. "For now, all I have is Izzy's Darklight gift."

She hefted the little packet. "Sweets? You think we can live on a tiny packet of sweets?"

"Of course not." I ground my teeth. She was misunderstanding me on purpose. "It's just a gift."

Running footsteps made us both look up just before a small figure barreled into me so hard she knocked me against the house wall. Lyssa tucked the packet of candy dust out of sight in her pocket.

"Hey there, Izzy." I pushed myself off the wall, feeling the start of the grin Izzy always provoked in me. She had the biggest brown eyes I'd ever seen on a kid. "I'm glad to see you too."

She looked me up and down, frowning. "Where's your wind box? I want you to read for me."

A knot formed in my stomach. "Are you the one who sent a messenger to me?"

She nodded. "I want to know what I'll get for Darklight."

Lyssa grabbed Izzy's shoulder and spun her around. "Izabeth! Where did you get the gull for the messenger?" Izzy looked at the cobblestones. Lyssa gave her a shake. "Don't touch the coins in the shop ever again, you hear?"

"Your ma's right." I felt giddy at what Clovyan might do if he caught Izzy filching coins. "Promise you won't."

"Oh, all right." Izzy scowled nearly as fiercely as Rena did.

Lyssa shook her head. "She's mad to know what her gifts will be. Tried to go to the castle all by herself and look for you."

I thought of Rena and the dead boy and went weak in

the knees.

Still scowling, Izzy took my free hand. "Ma said the Grabber would get me if I went to the castle again."

"He will," Lyssa said.

"He won't," Izzy said. "He's at the castle, but Jarka won't let him hurt me."

"Mind your ma," I said.

Izzy blinked at me, and I realized my tone had been sharp. "I mean it," I said.

She dropped my hand and turned to Lyssa. "I hope there's candy. Horehound is the best."

I blinked at her, then stared at Lyssa's pocket where she'd stowed my gift, my heart skipping around in my chest. When I read the wind in the castle cell, the little girl I sensed had tasted horehound. She'd been looking for me. Not Rena, I thought. The child I'd seen was Izzy.

I glimpsed movement over Lyssa's shoulder. "Look out!"

Clovyan grabbed Lyssa's arm and whirled her to face him. She shrieked, then clamped her mouth shut when she saw who it was. He loomed over her, face red, dark hair flopping into his eyes. Izzy trembled against my legs. At least I thought Izzy was the one shaking.

"What are you doing, woman?" Clovyan's voice was loud enough to push me back a step. He shook Lyssa, snapping her head back and forth. "I can't sew and tend the counter too. I came into the front room to see a customer walking away and you nowhere in sight. Now, I find you idling away with your know-it-all cousin." He glared at me, and even from where I stood, I saw the muscles in his forearms swell. My stomach tightened. "The boy might think he's one of the high and mighty, though I can tell him they'll toss him out of the castle the instant he causes trouble, but the rest of us still have to work if we want to eat."

"Jarka's just going," Lyssa said, "and I was only away for a moment."

"Don't argue with me!" Clovyan raised a hand. Lyssa flinched away and Clovyan's blow glanced off the top of her head.

Spots flickered through my vision. As if I had to push through molasses, I moved toward Clovyan. He pivoted and this time hammered his fist into the side of my head. I didn't even manage to get my arm up to block the punch.

I landed hard on the cobblestones, vision blurred, pain bursting in my ear and skull. The chickens squawked as if a cat had invaded their coop. Clovyan's face hovered over me. I felt his breath burning on my neck.

Over the frantic chickens, I heard Lyssa. "Don't hurt him, Clovyan. It was my fault. We should go back to the shop. What if there are customers there?"

Izzy's crying penetrated the roar in my ear. She strained against Lyssa's hold, trying to reach me.

"Let him be," Clovyan said. "And stop that noise, Izabeth." Izzy swallowed her sobs, but that didn't stop the tremor in her chin. Clovyan grabbed Lyssa's arm again.

"Come on, both of you, unless you want what he got." He hurried her off, still keeping hold of Lyssa.

Lyssa looked back over her shoulder. "Stay away, Jarka," she cried. Choosing Clovyan over me, the way she'd done the night he beat me bloody, the way she always did.

They vanished around the corner. A tiny white hen's feather floated to the ground at the tip of my nose.

I tried to get up, but my arm collapsed under me. I was going to have to wait for my strength to creep back with one side of my face pressed to the cobblestones and the other throbbing. Something warm slid down my cheek, and when I touched my nose, my fingers came away bloody. Clovyan's temper was even worse than I remembered, and that was saying a lot. All I had managed to do was provoke it. Clovyan was right. I might think I shared some of the castle's power, but the truth was I was as useless a joke as the Powers ever made.

# Chapter 9

I LIMPED ALONG with my gaze on the cobblestones—
light gray, dark gray, pitted, round. If I moved slowly
enough and gulped air, my vision stayed clear and
dizziness fluttered only at the edges of my head. I didn't
have to worry I'd run someone down. Three different folks
had taken sharp glances at me and veered out of my way.
My face throbbed, so it was probably already swelling and
turning blue, but I'd kept most of the blood from my nose
off my Wysman's apprentice shirt because I'd lain on the
street long enough for it to run off onto the cobblestones.
My hands were smeared, though, and probably my face
too. I'd wash them at the fountain in New Square before I
went back to the castle.

I'd be fine. Clovyan had hit me only once. But he
could so easily have hit Lyssa, have beaten her senseless.
She had a right to leave me unprotected. I wasn't a kid
anymore. But what was wrong with her that she didn't

leave him, didn't take Izzy clean out of Clovyan's reach? And what was wrong with me? I'd gone after Gelas in the cell, but facing Clovyan, I'd frozen and then been helpless to stop him from clobbering me.

The sun fell, warm on my face, and I looked up to find myself in the open space around New Square. I sank onto the edge of the fountain's lowest pool and plunged my hands into the water. A pink cloud swirled off them. I splashed my face, hoping the cold water would keep the swelling down. Adrya knew where I'd gone, so she'd know Clovyan hit me again, and I needed to convince her it wasn't so bad. Otherwise, she might tell me not to go back even if Lyssa did need me. Worse, she'd click her tongue and shake her head over "people like your cousin." Clovyan was right that castle folk—even the Wyswoman—almost all looked down on the rest of us, and not just because they lived at the top of the hill. Look at the way the king protected Rosin from punishment. Loyalty mattered more than a dead kid.

"You all right, Jarka?"

I blinked away water to see Timur frowning down at me. The left side of his face looked bruised, or was I just seeing what my own face probably looked like? I squinted, but Timur's bruise was still there. Not surprising really. Timur looked beat up pretty often.

Timur saw me looking and touched a finger to his face. "My granny said I was sniffling too much. Did someone at the castle hit you?"

"No. Clovyan."

Timur sat next to me, shoulders slumped. "Why do you go around there anyway?"

"Good question." Some nameless longing swelled in my throat. "I keep thinking I should do something to stop Clovyan from beating Lyssa up, or maybe talk her into leaving him and things would go back to the way they were before."

"If I had someplace else to stay, I wouldn't go back to my granny's." Timur dragged his sleeve under his nose.

I watched the Darklight wheels spinning between the top and middle levels of the fountain and again between the middle and bottom ones. I wished I could take Timur to the refuge, but he was too old, and besides, the refuge was full. What's more, given what happened to Rena, maybe the refuge wasn't the safest place after all. I wondered again how Rosin had got in. My stomach tightened. I was going to have to ask Ellyn if she locked the door.

"Next time you go to your cousin's, tell me, and I'll go with you to watch your back," Timur said.

"That's good of you, Timur."

He shrugged. "What are friends for?"

Timur's words latched on to that painful *want* in my throat. I pivoted to face him. "Actually, I could use a friend and not just with Clovyan. There's a guard at the castle who has it in for me. It would help me out if you could keep him off me." My brain spun like the Darklight wheels, working out how I could make this happen. Rosin had allies, including Adrya and Thien. I wanted one too. I needed one. And I trusted Timur. Timur and I had had the same kind of life. We understood one another. "If you mean it, I know a place you could stay for a few days anyway. That might give your granny time to—" I started to say "sober up" but changed it to "—cool down."

Timur straightened. "Where?"

"The castle. There's an empty bed in my dormitory room." The Powers' blessing on Dugan's family for moving him in with them. Maybe they'd made up for some of their crimes by leaving Dugan's bed for Timur.

"They'd let me stay?" Timur sounded breathless. "I'd work. I swear I would! I could run errands like I do now. I'm a good messenger."

I started to grin, but it made my face hurt. "The castle messengers are all little lordlings."

Timur punched my shoulder. "Go on with you."

"I should warn you there are bad things going on at the castle right now. A little girl's been hurt. Watching my back could be dangerous."

Timur waved his hand, chasing my warning away. "I've run into a lot of bad people, and none of them are more dangerous than my granny."

I thought about the dead boy and to my shame felt relief because his death far from the castle meant I could give in and let Timur come with me. I struggled to my feet. "We'll need a story, but I'll take care of that. Come on." I started up Kings Way, my head clearer and my heart lighter.

Timur surged ahead, then slowed to my pace. "You can come up with a story? You think this will work? I can stay in your room?"

I kept nodding, which was all right since Timur didn't wait for an answer anyway. The castle came in sight. "Hush now," I said. Timur clamped his mouth shut, but I heard his noisy breathing stop when we passed between the guards at the gate. One of the guards frowned at Timur's ragged clothes, which at least kept him from noticing any bruises I might be sprouting. "The first thing we need to do is get you cleaned up and into some castle clothes."

The courtyard was still busy with workers setting things up for the Darklight celebrations. A group of squires had propped one ladder against the stable and another against the kitchens so they could string white and black streamers along the eaves. The puppet show wagon had drawn up near the central fountain, and the puppeteers were joking together, lifting props out of a box on the wagon's open gate. I scanned the crowd for Gelas but didn't see him. I'd have to go after Rosin by myself because I promised Adrya to keep quiet about him, but if Timur could keep Gelas from cornering me somewhere, I'd feel a whole lot safer. Truth be told, I was embarrassed at how relieved the notion left me.

Timur's eyes darted from person to person, and he

scuttled behind me from shadow to shadow around the edge of the yard. He barely looked away from the swarm of workers even when he grabbed fistfuls of food from a table we passed. There were a lot of strangers in the yard, so one more was unlikely to draw attention, and folks were so busy they had no time to notice us anyway. Still my gut unknotted once we slipped through the castle door and found an empty hallway.

"Almost there," I said.

The dormitory hallway was empty too. I led Timur past the open curtains of other boys' rooms toward mine. I'd just realized my curtain was closed when a thud came from behind it, making me halt.

"Something the matter?" Timur pressed against my back.

"Maybe." I swept the curtain aside to find Dugan standing in the middle of the room looking straight at me. Stone the snot-mouthed rat. He was better than anyone I knew at turning up where he wasn't wanted. I hitched into the room, which was mine as much as his.

"Where'd you get the black eye?" Dugan frowned past me at Timur. "And who's he?"

Timur entered and put his back to the wall next to the doorway. His lips drew back, baring his teeth, surprisingly white against his bruised cheek.

I slid between them. "Timur came with some of the visiting nobles, and the castle's so full, he was supposed to stay in rooms over the stables, but there was a brawl there last night." I was talking too fast, like a seller of bad goods. I slowed down. "I helped him out in the fight, but we both got a little beat up, and now he needs a place to stay because he can't go back to the stables. The stable hands will be waiting for him."

"Does the dormitory master know about him?" Dugan asked.

"Of course," I lied. "Do you think I'd be gutsy enough to bring him in here if the master didn't know?"

"The old fool probably wouldn't notice he was a thug." Dugan wrinkled his nose. "He stinks."

I glanced over my shoulder. Streaks of something green ran down one side of Timur's shirt. His trousers were torn at one knee and gray with mud around the bottom. He stuffed his mouth with the last of the bread he'd picked up in the yard and chewed with his mouth open, all the while eyeing Dugan up and down as if deciding where to stick the shiv in. A flea hopped across his temple. He scratched its trail with a black fingernail.

I resisted the temptation to scratch my scalp. "He got knocked into horse droppings. I'm going to help him clean up. What are you doing here anyway?"

Dugan scanned the room, then snatched up the nightshirt he'd left under the washstand. When he straightened, he staggered. His face was pale, I realized. Like the stable boys, he'd probably had too much to drink the previous night. "Just getting this," he said. "I'm happy to leave though. It reeks in here." He batted the curtain aside and left.

Timur waited until Dugan's heavy footsteps dwindled. "I need a knife. I can lift one easy."

"No," I said hastily. "You can't lift anything while you're here."

Timur raised both eyebrows but said nothing.

I opened my clothes chest and rooted through it. Before Adrya took me on as an apprentice, Prince Beran gave me a plain black linen shirt and trousers. I found them at the bottom of the chest. They'd be too long on Timur, but he could roll up the trouser legs. I pulled them out, along with a set of underclothes, then glanced at the scraps of leather tied with string to his feet. I wore one normal shoe on my left foot and a special one made by the castle cobbler on my lame right one, so my chest didn't hold anything he could use. I poked the jumble under Dugan's bed, unearthed a pair of scuffed boots, and tossed them to Timur, who grinned widely.

"No lifting things. Right," he said.

"Dugan's stuff doesn't count. Come on. I'll show you where to wash." I led him back out, across the busy yard, and down a walkway to the baths. Compared to the castle side of the yard, this side made me think of Rin's slums, with their narrow alleys that housed the city's poorer folks, though of course poor was relative. The baths smelled of soap and steam. Behind me, Timur sniffed warily.

Inside the doorway, the attendant rose from his stool, eyes going from my bruises to Timur's. "Fight with the stable boys?" he asked.

I nodded, then jerked my thumb over my shoulder. "Timur doesn't have baths like this where he's from." The Powers only knew how true that one was. "You may need to show him how to use them." I thrust the pile of clean clothes into his arms.

He looked doubtfully at Timur. "What should I do with the clothes he's wearing?"

"Throw them away," I said.

"No," Timur said. "They're mine."

I hesitated. I still found it strange to have the castle laundresses washing my clothes. What would they make of Timur's raggedy shirt and trousers? It didn't matter, I decided, because Timur was right. A street kid needed to hang on to what was his. "Just put them in the dormitory laundry basket."

I turned to Timur. "I'll be back. If I'm not here when you finish, just go on out to the yard. Eat. Watch the puppet show." I leaned close so I could speak without the attendant hearing. "I'll point out the guard who's giving me trouble so you can keep an eye on him."

"Sure thing." His gaze flitted around the entryway, as if making sure nothing lurked in the corners. Hugging Dugan's boots to his chest, he followed the attendant down the hallway.

I set off to the infirmary to see how Rena was and maybe tell the healer what I sensed in her if he'd listen. Oh. And also ask Ellyn if she left the door open for Rosin. My stomach tightened. This would be tricky.

# Chapter 10

I HOBBLED INTO the infirmary in time to hear Ellyn say, "I found her before Jarka even got there." A small crowd was gathered around one of the cots lining each side of the room. They all turned to see who'd come in, and I rocked back. I'd expected the healer and Ellyn, of course, but not Lady Lineth sitting next to the unconscious Rena with Laren on her lap. And definitely not Gelas, who stood on the near side of the bed, petting his baby moustache, and facing off with the rest of them on the other side. I glanced over my shoulder at the door. Maybe I should have waited until Timur was ready.

"Jarka!" Ellyn had been standing with one hand on the hilt of her knife but now her shoulders relaxed. "I was worried when you didn't show up for so long." The space between her eyebrows puckered. "What happened to your face?" She moved close enough to lay a gentle finger on my cheek. I froze.

"Yes." Gelas turned to face me, eyes narrowed. "What have you been doing?"

Ellyn dropped her hand, and I struggled out of my daze. "It's not castle business," I said. No way was I going to lay my family troubles out for this guard to pick over.

He took a step toward me. "I asked what you've been up to."

"And I said it wasn't your business." He raised his hands as if to seize me, and I embarrassed myself by adding, "Ask the gate guards. They'll tell you I left the castle." I waved toward my throbbing face. "This had nothing to do with Rena."

Laren let out a low, hopeless wail. "The Grabber got her."

"Hush, sweetness." Lineth stroked his hair and pulled him against her.

The healer stalked around the cot. "You're not going to learn any more, Gelas, and you're upsetting my patients. Get out of my infirmary."

Gelas held his ground long enough to make the healer take another step. Then he gave way. As he brushed past me, he said, "I'm not done with you." He shut the door hard behind him. The sick feeling in my gut eased.

The healer turned me to face the windows so I squinted into the afternoon sun. He smelled of liniment, and the skin of his fingers was slightly rough. He scrutinized my face, then prodded my ear. I jerked away. "Is there a roaring in that ear?" he asked.

"No." *Not much.* "What did Gelas want?"

Before the healer could answer, Ellyn cut in. "He says you ensorcelled Rena, and he wanted everyone else to agree." She looked ready to fall over. Everything about her drooped. The dress she still wore seemed to bag around her. At least, the knife cut on her arm was now wrapped in a bandage.

The healer turned to study Rena, lying motionless as a wax doll. "It might be sorcery for all I know. I've never seen anything like this."

I drew near enough to put a hand on Rena's shoulder. Someone, probably Lineth, had fetched her nightgown, and right through the linen, her skin felt cold. I hesitated because I didn't want to point a finger at myself, but maybe knowing the truth would help the healer cure Rena. "There's no such thing as sorcery. Someone's tried to use elemental power on her and mucked it up, which might be a good thing. Better than what he intended anyway."

Ellyn withdrew her knife a finger's width and then slid it home with a snap. "The Grabber may be a fright tale, but what's in this castle is frightening enough. That guard didn't care about Rena. He just wants to prove it was you who hurt her."

The healer shot me a sharp look. "Do you how to remedy whatever is wrong?" When I shook my head, he ran his long fingers through his wispy hair. "I'll keep Rena here then. Maybe Adrya will be able to find some wisdom in the library."

Lineth rose and tried to settle Laren on her hip, but he arched his back and tried to fling himself off her. "No! No! Gonna stay with Rena."

"Don't worry, Laren." Ellyn's voice shook. She began gathering Rena up, blanket and all. "She's not staying in this castle another hour. I'm taking her home. You can send word to the refuge if you learn how to help her."

The healer laid a hand on her arm. "Wait. If you're determined, I can't stop you, but let me get my assistant to carry her. You belong in bed yourself." He started toward a door at the other end of the room, but stopped next to Lineth, to whom Laren now clung. "You too, lady, by the look of you."

Lineth did look tired, I realized, though next to Ellyn it was hard to notice. She seemed to feel the pressure of Ellyn's eyes and mine, because she blinked at us and spoke to Laren. "Shall we go and make sure Rena's bed is ready for her at home?" He twisted to look at his sister, and I could see his body tightening. "We can push your bed up next to it," Lineth said, and finally he nodded. Lineth wasted no time whisking him out of the infirmary.

A tall healer's apprentice came from the back of the room, collected Rena in his arms, and asked, "Are you ready?" Without waiting for our answer, he strode away leaving Ellyn and me to scramble after him along a winding castle hallway that eventually led to the courtyard door.

"Slow down," I said to Ellyn. She glanced at my crutch

and obliged. My face burned, but the healer's apprentice surged far enough ahead that I could talk to her without him hearing.

"I've been wondering how whoever took Rena got into the refuge." I hated to do it now when my face still tingled where Ellyn touched me, but I had to be sure they'd all be safe in the refuge. I drew a deep breath. "Did you leave the door unlocked?"

She sucked in her breath. "Of course not!"

"So they were all locked in?" That didn't make me happy either.

She stopped walking entirely. Ahead of us, I glimpsed the healer's apprentice shoving through the door to the yard. "No." She jutted her chin at me. "That would be a very bad idea. What if there was a fire or someone needed help? I used the spare key."

"Oh, good." The muscles in my shoulders softened. "I didn't know there was a second key."

She pursed her lips. "We're not fools, Jarka. We can recognize danger without you pointing it out."

"Sorry."

Her tense face relaxed a little. "Lady Lineth had the extra key made in case someone needed to get in without notice. We keep it in a hollow under the front step."

I flung up my free hand. "What? Anyone could find it there."

"Well, they didn't. It was still there this morning when Lineth went to fetch Laren." She sped toward the door the healer had gone through with me trailing after.

"But someone could have used it and put it back."

"Stop accusing me, Jarka." She was ahead of me, so I couldn't see her face, but her voice trembled.

"How else could someone have got hold of Rena?"

"I don't know, but not that." She pushed the door open to the sunny courtyard where the puppet show was underway, looked over her shoulder, and flung words at me like weapons. "I'm tired. Leave me alone."

I trailed her into the yard and watched her all but run through the crowd and out the gate, swiping at the tears I'd seen on her cheeks. *Stone it, stone it, stone it.* I leaned against the sun-warmed wall next to the door and took a moment to close my eyes. This day had already gone on forever. A kid had been left half dead, riddled with bad power by a man Adrya and the king protected. For the first time in my life, I'd landed in a cell, thrown there by a guard who wanted to bleed the wind reading out of me. Definitely *not* for the first time Clovyan had knocked the crap out of me. Ellyn balanced somewhere between scared of me and furious at me for accusing her of carelessness, which to be fair, I had. It occurred to me that given her brother vanishing from under her nose, that must have hurt more than I'd meant it to. Too late to do anything about that now. The only thing that would fix any of that was finding evidence against Rosin and doing it within three days. If I managed that, Ellyn would forgive me. She might even admire the cleverness it took to do that. All my life, I'd used my sharp mind to balance my crooked body. I could do that again. I opened my eyes, got my crutch under me, and scanned the courtyard.

Kids crowded around the puppet cart while their parents or, since these were castle kids, their nannies watched from farther back. It took me a moment to recognize a boy from the refuge and then realize the rest of them were there too, hanging back behind the castle kids and watched over by Tally. She kept spreading her arms out wide as if to be sure they were corralled where they should be. On my right, a silk clad woman spoke to the man next to her. "Why are those urchins allowed in?"

"I gather Lady Lineth asked for it," the man said.

"That girl will never keep control of them. They're too rough."

I "accidentally" tripped and pinned the edge of her skirt under my crutch to catch myself. "Sorry," I said when she jumped with the satisfying sound of silk ripping.

On the stage, a puppet squirrel ran frantically from side to side, arms full of honeyed nuts, begging someone to tell him where to hide them from the bear cub who was sure to steal them. The audience shouted advice. Beyond them, my eye caught on a vaguely familiar, hollow-cheeked boy leaning against the stable, taking huge bites of one of the black and white Darklight cakes being served on the yard's edges. The boy lifted his hand in greeting, and I realized it wasn't the boy who looked familiar. It was the clothes. They were mine. The Powers save me. That clean, well-brushed boy was Timur. I worked my way through the crowd toward him. The kids in the audience were jumping up and down because now the squirrel and the bear cub wrestled over the honey-coated nuts, and they, like everyone else here, knew what happened next in this play. Sure enough, eager to smack one another, the puppets flung the nuts into the audience, and kids dove for them, their shrieks bouncing off the walls. The refuge kids threw themselves into the fray with elbows flying to knock rivals out of the way. One of them rammed my crutch, and I had to scramble. The woman who worried they'd be trouble was probably screeching, but I couldn't hear her over the rioting kids.

I washed up next to Timur, who was clearly twitching to grab a few nuts. I had to admit I was tempted too. The habit of storing up against hungry days was hard to break. "How are you doing?" I asked.

The scrum over the nuts had died down, and Timur's unblinking gaze had locked onto someone on the other side of the yard. Dugan, I realized, sitting on a bench next to his mother. He looked straight ahead while she spoke into his ear, gesturing sharply at the crowd in the yard.

"Your roommate's a rich kid. How come he acts like life did him dirt and it's our fault?"

Dugan slid a few inches away from Brylla's still moving mouth. "Good question." But since trying to answer might force me to feel some sympathy for Dugan, I ignored it, which was easy because at that moment, Gelas emerged from the guard barracks. "See that guard over there? He's the one who's after me. Name of Gelas."

Timur's eyes swept down and up, taking in every detail of Gelas' appearance. He snorted. "My granny looks tougher."

"Your granny didn't come after anyone with a knife this morning."

Timur said nothing. I gave him a sideways glance and let the matter drop. Gelas skirted the crowd and vanished into the castle.

"Hey, Timur." A boy from the refuge stopped in front of us, utterly unfazed to see Timur in the yard. Timur nodded a greeting while his puzzled gaze went back to Dugan, and the kid turned to me. "A man was here carrying Rena. Did the Grabber take her to the castle?"

"Someone did," I said soberly.

He hugged himself, jamming his hands in his armpits. "Did he take her to the cave with the well?" He glanced around the yard, body rigid.

One street kid to another, I knew what he was thinking as clearly as if he'd said it out loud. Rena and Laren had already run away from the refuge because half the parents in the city scared their kids into behaving by telling them the Grabber's hill was the one on which the castle stood. It wouldn't take much to make this kid bolt, and maybe others too. "She's going to be all right now that she's home. And don't worry. I'll keep the Grabber away from you all. I'm the one who found you, remember? I wouldn't want to lose you now."

He nodded and started to turn away but stopped to ask, "Does your face hurt?"

"Not much." *Like I was kicked by a mule.*

He trotted to join the crowd of rowdy kids Tally was shepherding out the gate, all of them gleefully shoving honeyed nuts into their mouths.

"Who's Rena?" Timur raised his arm, ready to drag the sleeve of his—my—shirt under his dripping nose. He stopped, glanced down at the clean clothes, and pulled a handkerchief I didn't recognize out of a pocket.

"A little girl from the refuge. The one you saw in New Square. She's the one somebody hurt."

"Somebody from the castle?"

"Yeah, and I'm going to prove who it was while you keep Gelas off my back." Something about the refuge boy's question nagged in my head. Every version of the Grabber tale I'd ever heard said he lived in a cave and was dropping a kid into water when the mother came to the rescue. Rena's clothes had been wet, and I'd assumed they'd been soaked when the fountain blew up, but maybe they'd been wet before she was abandoned in the yard. I stared at the fountain, seeing again how water had flooded the yard. Could a well be part of how Rosin's uncle had worked the magic? I turned the idea over and took a good look. "You ever hear of a cave or a well on castle hill?" I asked. Timur shook his head. A wisp of memory floated loose. I'd read or heard of something called a well of sharing. Was that connected or just what you'd expect a commonly shared well to be called?

I beat the end of my crutch against the flagstones. I needed more information. My wind box would at least have been a good place to start looking for it. I watched people drifting toward the castle entry, eager for their supper. There'd be workers still in the yard and outbuildings, though, the ones who routinely had night duty. With Gelas at supper, it would be a good time to ask if they'd seen Rosin the night before and knew where he'd been.

"Are you still hungry?" I asked Timur.

He blinked at me as if he couldn't make out the words.

"There's supper in the Hall," I said, making his eyes widen. "I'll show you where to sit and then come back out. I want to question people out here."

He rocked from foot to foot. "I'll stay with you and keep an eye out."

Timur offering to miss a meal was possibly the most heroic thing anyone had ever offered to do for me. "You don't have to. Gelas is inside."

His gaze slid over my shoulder, and he edged away.

"What happened to your face?" an unwelcome voice asked.

Adrya frowned at me. I couldn't give her the stable boy fight story because she'd seen me this morning after it'd happened. We'd heard and smelled the stable boys puking in the jail. I groped for an excuse but she saved me the trouble. "Your cousin's husband." Her mouth pinched around the words. Her guess didn't surprise me. She knew where I'd been headed when I left her. I half expected her to forbid me going to Lyssa's again, but she only said, "Come inside."

"I'm not hungry. I've been eating stuff in the yard all day."

"I don't care. I want you next to me at supper." She strode off toward the castle, leaving a trail of flowery perfume. "Flowers," Rena had said. The Grabber smelled "like flowers."

I froze for a moment before I thought *not possible*. I glanced over my shoulder at Timur. "Later," I mouthed. He nodded and sped inside, beating me to the Hall and finding his own way to the food.

# Chapter 11

I INCHED TOWARD the door, setting the tip of my crutch carefully on the floor of the dormitory hallway. The master's room was at the end, his door standing ajar as it did every night. I could hear him snoring, but every boy in the dorm knew he was a light sleeper. What's more, while he left the entry door unlocked, he padlocked a chain of bells to it at night. We'd all been awakened by him shouting at boys coming in after curfew. I eased his door shut. Timur edged up next to me, and we stared at the chain of three bells dangling from a loop bolted to the door. I held out my hand, but nothing appeared in it, and when I glanced at Timur, he clutched the chunk of dinner bread I'd saved to his chest. "There'll be more tomorrow," I whispered. His fingers slowly uncurled and he laid it on my palm. I pinched some off and stretched, meaning to wad it around the tongue of a bell. The other two tinkled softly, and I drew back.

"Let me." Timur took the bread and with a touch whose delicacy I could only admire, he muffled all three of them before popping the padlock. I breathed a sigh of relief that the bit of bread I jammed in the lock earlier had held and kept the shank from latching. Once out in the castle hallway, we kept to the shadows, heading for the courtyard. "That's a good trick," Timur said admiringly. "I never could have thought of it. I thought we'd just go out the window."

"We're on the third floor."

He shrugged. "We could climb down."

I tightened my grip on my crutch and shut my mouth. Some things, you could rely on Timur for. Some things, you couldn't.

"So what are we doing?" he asked.

"First, I want to question the guards and anyone else who works at night about whether they saw Rosin going after Rena. Gelas will be on duty by now. Can you keep a lookout for him? The old keep is his territory."

We slid out into the torchlit yard. Timur ghosted toward the entry into the keep, and I hobbled the other way along, circling the edge toward the gate. From mornings reading the wind, I knew the middle of the yard was visible on the keep wall. So was the gate, for that matter, but that couldn't be helped. Gelas would mostly be watching for trouble approaching from outside, but he'd be checking for castle troublemakers roaming in the dark too. Not that I meant to make trouble. I wanted to find evidence of Rosin's guilt in as trouble-free a way as possible.

The gate was closed for the night and only a single guard stood in the passage running through the wall from it to the yard. He was leaning against the wall, but when I stepped into the passage, he snapped erect until he saw who it was and relaxed. He must have been bored because he answered my questions readily.

Yes, he'd been on duty during the dancing. Yes, the gates had been left open much later than usual. Town nobles arrived and left the party, and some of the out-of-town visitors lodged in town because there were too many for the castle to accommodate or they owned houses there. He and the guard who'd been on duty with him checked everyone who entered against a guest list, and only people on it were allowed through. I knew someone had let Ellyn through at dawn but I didn't ask him about that. She wasn't the one I was worried about, and I knew Rosin and Brylla were staying in the castle.

"How about when people leave?" I asked. "Do you keep a record of that?"

"No. Why would we?"

"Did you happen to notice if Lord Rosin left?"

The guard pursed his lips and thought for a moment, scanning a scene in his head. "Big fellow? Convinced of his own charm? Yes, I think he did." My breath caught, but before I could press for details, he added, "I noticed because he had his arm around a woman whose hood was pulled forward to hide her face. Not his wife would be my guess." He rolled his eyes. "Nobles. My wife would come after me with the poultry shears."

I chewed the inside of my cheek. "Do you know who she was?"

He shrugged. "Not my business."

So I couldn't ask her when Rosin left her. "Did he come back later, maybe with a child?"

He was already shaking his head. "When we opened the gate in the morning, he was waiting outside. Strolled in like a tomcat that's been out all night. Pleased with himself."

Stone it. "Did anyone come in with a child?"

"Not that I saw."

I turned away, trying to figure out what to do next. I'd meant to ask other night workers if they'd seen Rosin, but the guard was so definite there seemed no point. Rosin had left the castle and not come back until I saw him in the morning, which meant he couldn't have dumped Rena in the yard. He must have worked it some way I hadn't figured out yet.

I retraced my steps around the yard, meaning to retrieve Timur for our second mission of the night, one I hoped would give me some insight. Before I got to the keep entry though, a man shouted, "Wait! You!" and Timur sped into sight.

"We should go." He grabbed my upper arm, half dragged me through the nearest door, and shoved me into the shadows behind one of the pillars scattered apparently randomly through the twisty castle hallways.

"What—"

"Shh." He tucked something small into his pocket. I saw again the delicate touch he'd used on the bells and smothered a groan.

I heard the door we'd come through open, and cool night air chilled the sweat that had sprung out on my neck. Next to me, Timur's usual noisy breathing stopped.

"A skinny boy, you say?" Gelas' voice was stomach churningly near on the other side of the pillar.

"I think so," a man said. "It was dark."

"Are you sure he came this way?"

"Once he ran out of the keep, I couldn't see him."

"There's no one here."

Steps moved away, and the door thumped shut. The breath Timur had been holding exploded out of him, ruffling the hair over my right ear.

"You really can't lift things in the castle," I said.

"Maybe it wasn't me."

I snorted.

"Did I wreck what we were doing?" he asked anxiously.

"Not really. That was a dead end. I have another thing to do though, and for that, we need to go to the library."

"We're going to read?" He braced himself against the pillar like he might fall over at the ridiculousness of the idea.

"No. Adrya took my wind box. We're going to take it back."

He bared his teeth. "No lifting things in the castle, though."

"It's mine," I said. And not just mine, but *me*. It was the source of my power, the reason I was in the castle, the way I understood the energy throbbing through the world. "Street rules for that."

He nodded.

THE HALLWAY OUTSIDE the library was dark. "You think she's keeping it in there?" Timur asked.

"I hope so. I really don't want to have to search her quarters."

Timur fingered whatever he'd hidden in his pocket and cocked his head thoughtfully.

"Whatever you're thinking, stop," I said. "You wait out here. Warn me if someone comes." I crept to the door and eased it open. As I expected, no one was there, but a book lay open on the table. Stone Adrya. Did she never sleep? I slipped inside and shut the door. If she'd left a book out, she'd be back.

The lamp was gone from the table but enough torchlight from the yard filtered through the open window for me to see that the book was a herbal, open to a remedy that would 'call the spirit back to the body.' I started to tilt the book to catch the light better but snatched my hand back and shook my fingers. The book throbbed with misshapen power. Slowly, I swiveled to contemplate the shelves in the corner of the room. Adrya might say Rosin didn't know how to mischannel water, but it had just occurred to me that yesterday I'd seen a way he could have learned by reading. Not well enough to carry out his goal and leave Rena a shriveled body like Ellyn's brother, but just enough to leave her lost somewhere inside her body. If Rosin cared enough, though, he'd try again.

Adrya's determination to keep me from my wind box and news of her "old friend" Rosin set my teeth on edge. She'd mostly treated me well, but trust came as hard to me as it did to Timur. The box wasn't sitting around where I could see it. Moving quickly, I started at one end of a row of cupboards and yanked doors open. My carry bag slumped behind the third one. I lifted the flap to make sure, but I knew the moment I touched it that the wind box was inside. I stroked one of the rune-carved pieces, then retied the flap and carried it to the door.

Timur slithered around the corner the instant I opened the door. I handed him the bag. "Hide this in our room."

"Now? Aren't you coming?"

"Soon. I have something to do first."

"You'll be all right without me?"

"Yes. Go." Without waiting to see if he obeyed, I shut the door and hustled to the corner shelves where Adrya had stowed the book that quivered with dark power. That was where I'd seen the reference to the Well of Sharing. And there'd been an incantation. I grabbed the step stool in passing, set it firmly in front of the shelf, and climbed onto the lower step. Now came the tricky part. I leaned my crutch against a row of books, clutched a shelf and carefully pulled myself up onto the upper step. Balancing on one foot, I pawed through the books on the topmost shelf. Two of them had the same feel as the book I'd found earlier, the same feel as the herbal on the table. But the one I was looking for was gone. To be sure, I pulled out first one of the darkness-tinged books and then the other. I was sliding the second one back into place when my gaze caught on the cover. It was marked with a stone arch like the book with the reference to The Well of Sharing. Not an arch, I realized. A bridge. A stone bridge. My pulse thundered in my ears. The book I wanted wasn't here, but I was sure I knew who had taken it. I shoved the book back into line, fury flooding me. I knew it. Stone it. I knew it.

Something creaked on one side of the fireplace, and Adrya entered the room where no door existed. Surprised into a yelp, I felt myself tipping backward and grabbed the shelf too late. My back hit the floor, followed an instant later by my skull. All the breath was knocked out of me. The pain in my head was blinding.

"Jarka!" Adrya bent over me. "Are you all right?"

"Yes," I managed to squeak.

She reached to help me up and handed me my crutch.

"What are you doing here?" she demanded.

"Looking for a book. Never mind me. What are you doing here?" I limped over to stare at what now looked like just a rune-covered wall. "Is that a door?" I gave the panel an experimental push, but it stayed still, solid as the stretch of wall it seemed to be.

"You won't be able to open it, so you might as well leave it alone." Adrya glanced at the cupboard where my wind box had been hidden and was apparently content that its closed door and my empty hand meant it was still safely there. She thumped the oil lamp she'd been carrying onto the table and seated herself. "And if you want to continue to be my apprentice, you must swear not to tell anyone of its existence."

"But what is it?" I followed her to the table. "Where does it go?"

"To passages where only Wysones are allowed, which means you're not ready to use it yet." She frowned at me. "Why aren't you in the dorm?"

"I couldn't sleep. You said passages? More than one?" A staggering thought dropped me onto the stool across from her. "You're spying on folks in the castle. That's how you always know how to aim your interpretation at morning prayers."

"I am not 'spying.'" Adrya snapped out each word, lifting her shoulders like a bird ruffling its feathers. "I am merely gathering information so I can advise my king, as is my obligation."

"Does Thien know about the passages?"

She shifted in her chair. "No. The knowledge is passed from Wysone to Wysone right here in this library."

"They lead to peepholes or places you can listen?" My mind skittered over an image of Rosin when he didn't know an outsider might be listening and looking. I burned to tell her what I believed Rosin had done with the missing book, but she'd made it clear I was to stay away from him. A nasty suspicion sprang to life that she already knew and that was why she'd snatched the book and the wind box away from me.

"They lead elsewhere in the castle," she said, "and that's all you need to know." She pulled the herbal toward her, then wiped her hands on her skirt.

"Something wrong with the herbal?" I shifted my gaze from her hands to her face.

"No." She frowned at the page. "The healer asked me to search for any knowledge that might help the little girl from the refuge."

"You don't sense something off about that book when you touch it?"

"Of course not." Adrya stretched so erect, she quivered. "Only the ignorant believe there's something unnatural about a book, and that's when they end up burning it."

"That book might not be the best one to use if you're truly concerned about Rena," I said, keeping my voice even.

She clutched her Wyswoman pendant. "I know you think I'm indifferent to her, but you're wrong. It's just that the king can't allow the fate of one person to disrupt the relations he has with his lords."

"Every person in Rinland is just one person." Bitterness churned in my belly. "If there's no justice for them, then why should they care about Thien and his lords?"

"You've never seen the country at war," Adrya said. "There's not much I wouldn't do to keep something like that from happening again."

"Good to know." I shoved to my feet.

"I'll see you at prayers," she said.

I left the library without looking back.

I ENTERED MY room to find Timur already in Dugan's bed. He'd folded his borrowed clothes and draped them carefully over the bottom of the bed frame.

"Things all right?" he asked.

"As right as they're going to be." I stripped and pulled on my nightshirt. What I could see of Timur told me he was naked under the covers.

I barely had time to climb into my own bed before the dormitory door opened hard enough that the bells sounded dully even in their bread-covered state. Someone banged on a door, and I heard the dormitory master cry,

"What is it?"

The answer came in Gelas' voice. "Sorry. We had a thief in the yard earlier and now there's been a report that one of your charges stole a book. I have to search his belongings. Where's Adrya's apprentice?"

Bare feet whispered down the hall, followed by booted ones. The curtain swept aside, and Gelas stood there next to the sleepy looking dormitory master. Gelas stepped inside.

"Move," he told me.

I could hear boys stirring in other rooms and curtain rings clanking. I slid out of bed and edged away, completely confused. Had Adrya realized the Well of Sharing book was missing, gone to Gelas, and named me as the thief? If so, she'd been fast. I felt the beginnings of outrage at the betrayal.

Gelas yanked all the blankets off my bed, then crouched to look underneath. Nose wrinkled, he pulled my carry bag out from where Timur had evidently shoved it. He unwound the tie, looked inside, and dropped the bag on the wrecked bed. At least, he didn't know the box was supposed to be in Adrya's hands.

"Is this your chest?" he asked. When I nodded, he flung the top up and rooted through, leaving it too a mess. Finally, he straightened and turned to Timur, who sat with his back against the wall and his covers over his lap. Mercifully, Gelas did not order Timur out of bed. "Where's your chest?"

"I'm a visitor," Timur offered.

"The space over the stables was full," I said.

"Someone should have told me." The dormitory master smoothed his sleep mussed hair, but his nightshirt undercut his attempt at dignity.

"You can ask Lady Lineth," I said.

"Satisfied?" The master vented his irritation on Gelas. "Now that you've upset everyone?" The master stepped back, obviously inviting Gelas to leave, which Gelas did, though his step was slow. I stayed where I was until the door closed behind him, then started heaving covers back onto my bed.

"Here." Lifting a hip, Timur pulled something out from under his butt. He held it out to me. "Your book fell out when I hid the box."

"Fell out from where?" I stared stupidly at what was in his hand.

"Under your mattress."

I took the book from him and instantly dumped it on my bed. It throbbed with bad power. When it landed, the book fell open to show an incantation headed "For the Well of Sharing."

# Chapter 12

I STARED AT the book, my mind racing. Someone had told Gelas I stole it. The same someone had planted it to make it look as if *I* were the one who'd used dark power to hurt Rena. Gelas already believed that. Other people would too. Who looked more likely to be guilty—a street kid who read the wind or one of Thien's lords? Adrya and Thien knew Rosin had benefitted from hurting a kid before, but I wasn't at all sure they'd come down on the right side. "There's not much I wouldn't do," Adrya had said.

"Is something wrong?" Timur asked.

"A lot is wrong." Now that I had the book, I wasn't sure what to do with it. I sure didn't intend to use any of what was in it. I skimmed my gaze down the incantation and my stomach turned over. *My heart leaps with power. I open my hand and let my power go.* "For now, though, we're going to hide this and get some sleep." I glanced around for a likely hiding place.

"Put it back under your mattress," Timur said. "It's good to use a place they already looked."

I did as he suggested. Some things you couldn't rely on Timur for. This was one of the things you could.

I CAME OUT of prayers the next morning expecting to find Timur waiting for me in the back hallway ready to help me find a place to safely use my wind box. He was there at the far end, silhouetted against the light from the open courtyard door, but between him and me, Lineth stood stiffly, half-turned away from Rosin. At the sight of the man, hot fury bubbled in my chest. I stopped. I'd promised Adrya I'd stay away from him on pain of being locked in a cell where Gelas could find me.

"But I've been told you're free to make a different choice." Rosin leaned toward Lineth. "You and His Highness don't plan to defy his father over this, do you?"

Lineth looked straight ahead and spoke loudly enough that Rosin blinked. "His Highness and I are completely loyal to His Majesty."

"Perhaps Beran's loss can be someone else's gain." Rosin tried to sidle into her line of view, but she turned her head. I knew the instant she caught sight of me because the tension in her body loosened. She beckoned to me. Rosin glanced my way and stepped back from her.

"Think on what I've said, my dear." He bowed to her and strolled off. In the doorway, Timur stepped aside, hands up, palms out as if to show they were empty of any coins, weapons, or jewelry Rosin might have on his person, so Rosin had plenty of room, but he turned sideways to slip past him. Timur moved a toe toward me but stayed where he was when Lineth laid a hand on my arm.

"Jarka, I'm sorry to bother you, but I wonder if you'd be willing to read the wind for me."

Sometimes the Powers gave a street kid a break after all. "Of course. There's a problem though. Gelas, that guard in the infirmary? He won't let me read on the walkway."

She fingered a tiny lump under her bodice, probably the charm she wore. "My room has a balcony. It's on the fourth floor. Would that work?"

"We can try. I'll get my box."

"Thank you." She pressed a palm to her chest and heaved a deep breath. "Is Gelas bothering you? Beran asked me to make sure you were well-treated while he was gone. The king won't see me, but I could ask Adrya to intervene."

"Don't do that," I said hastily. "I'm fine."

"Good. Let me know if there's a problem." She walked at my side toward where stairs led up. With one foot on the second step, she looked back. "Aren't you coming?"

"In a moment. You go ahead."

As soon as she was gone, Timur came to meet me.

"Did you hear that?" I asked. "I'll read for her and then for me. I'll find you in the yard once I have an idea of what to do next. I hear there are treats again."

He was speeding toward the yard before I'd finished speaking.

ON THE THIRD-FLOOR landing, I clutched my carry bag and stepped aside to let a trio of silk-clad young women pass. I recognized one from having read the wind for her. She nodded to me, but the others were busy talking about a man they both found "delicious." I chose not to wonder what that meant. As their voices dwindled, I looked up the stairs. The boys' dorm was on this floor, and I'd never climbed beyond it because that territory belonged to single women. When I heard no more voices, I hurried up, stretching to see that the corridor was empty before I went up the last few steps. I knocked on the door Lineth had said was hers. It opened at once, and Lineth waved me inside.

Once I moved into the castle, I'd figured out that, like in the street, the size of your territory showed how high you rated in the pecking order, and I hadn't been sure what kind of space a traitor nobleman's daughter merited. Lineth's territory had no separate sitting room, but it was large with embroidered hangings on the bed and a silver pitcher on the washstand. I sniffed. Underneath the smell

146

of wax polish, a sour tang lingered. I glanced at Lineth. Maybe she really had felt sick at the dance.

Oblivious to my concern, Lineth led me out onto a balcony overlooking the river. At once, a breeze stirred the hair on my temples. "Will this do?" She twisted her hands together.

"Bless you, lady. It will do just fine." I fumbled with my bag, eager to get the box out and set it up on the stool she had ready. Wind wrapped around me. *Secrets*, it breathed. *Hurry*. With a trembling hand, I offered her the bag of paper bits.

She opened the bag, but then stopped, biting her lip. "I apologize if this sounds rude, Jarka, but do I have to ask my question out loud?"

*Secrets.*

"You're not the first to ask that. You have to speak your question, but you can whisper so I don't hear. I won't understand the answer as well though."

A faint line between her brows, she stared into the box. I'd just about decided she was going to back out when she dumped the paper into her palm and nodded at me to say the incantation.

I began. "The Powers move in the wind." She flung four scatterings of paper, then blew on them. I took a step back and looked away, but from the corner of my eye I saw her bend close and murmur into the box. She straightened and waited for me to give her answer with her fingers on the charm under her bodice.

I looked at the paper drifting like snow in the wind. Feelings that weren't mine swept up from my chest into my throat. My heart drove through a layer of worry and leapt, wild with joy, like a gull soaring toward the sun. I blinked. Lady Lineth waited with parted lips. "I think the answer makes you happy," I said.

She leaned against the castle wall and closed her eyes. Slowly, her mouth bent into a smile. "Thank you, Jarka." She straightened and stood there, obviously waiting for me to pack up.

"Would you mind if I read for myself?" I asked.

"Of course not. I should have thought of that." She stepped into her room, closing the balcony door. Through the glass, I saw her sit on the bed and stare off into nowhere. I was glad the reading was welcome because I'd found not all secrets were good ones. Like Rosin's, for instance.

I gathered up the paper and flung it back, repeating what I'd done for Lineth, only this time, I was the one leaning close to ask my question. "How did Rosin get Rena into the castle?" Wind swirled the paper in lazy spirals, ignoring me, so I tried a question that had come to me during the night. "Did Rosin bring her through one of the passages Adrya uses?" Wind threw paper bits into my face. I backed away, snorting out what I'd inhaled and blinking bits from my eyelashes. I tried, "Where did Rosin find Rena?"

The wind box, the balcony, the river beyond all faded.

I swaggered into a room where a pretty young woman stood to greet me. Other people hovered around me, but I ignored them. They were nobodies. This woman was worth appreciating though. And of course, now that she'd seen me, she'd appreciate me back. "Lord Rosin," Lineth said. "Thank you for visiting the refuge."

A breeze puffed into my face, and I stumbled for balance, once again on Lineth's balcony in the castle. I shook my head to clear it. That was a meeting I'd been present for two days ago when I took Rena and Laren back to the refuge, meaning I'd learned nothing new. The paper bits lay still in the bottom of the box. The wind had told me what it meant to for now. I'd been too stoning stupid to ask the right questions. No wonder other folks thought my gift was useless. Wind reading was only as insightful as the reader was, and now when it counted, I'd been blind. All right then. I'd use whatever wits I could scrounge up. Rosin was not getting away with harming Rena. I stowed everything back in my carry bag and joined Lineth in her room. "Would it be all right if I left my bag here?"

She cocked her head but simply said, "Of course."

I tucked it out of the way in a corner. Sooner or later, Adrya would notice the wind box was gone from her cupboard. She'd guess I took it but have no way to prove it if I didn't set it up in public. I kept running my mind over the scene the wind had shown me. Rosin found Rena at the refuge. Could the wind be suggesting he'd found her there again after that first visit?

"Lady, when you went to the refuge to get Laren yesterday morning, was the extra key under the steps where it belonged?"

"I don't know," Lineth said. "Tally had already opened the door from the inside."

That wasn't what Ellyn had told me, but then she hadn't been there.

"Would you have been able to tell if the key had been taken and put back?"

"I doubt it. Are you thinking someone took it and got into the refuge? We should find a different hiding place. Maybe under the flower pot on the window sill."

"That might be too easy to guess." Any city householder who had a flower pot probably hid their key under it. Lyssa and Clovyan did.

Her brow puckered. "I'm going to the refuge now to conduct lessons. Can you come and pick out a better place?"

I pictured Ellyn the last time I'd seen her, telling me to stop accusing her of carelessness, to leave her alone. She'd be even angrier if I showed up still harping on the key.

"Unless Adrya expects you," Lineth said after a moment.

"No. She freed me for the holiday and went off to the library on her own." Which was why I hadn't yet tried to open the door to the passages by myself, though it was still on my chore list. "I'll come with you. I want to search the refuge for any sign that an outsider got in. And maybe

Rena's come back to herself enough to speak a little." If Ellyn was angry at me for thinking Rosin had used the key to get into the refuge, so be it. Rosin would go home in two days. Time was running short.

I followed Lineth down four flights and out into the yard where Darklight games were underway. Women were racing around the fountain and back to the starting place, their teeth clenching egg-balancing spoons. Around the edges, people cheered them on.

Timur must have been watching for me because he trotted over at once, a half-eaten Darklight cake clutched in one hand. He shoved the rest in his mouth. "You need me?" he mumbled around it.

One eyebrow raised, Lineth looked from me to him.

"This is Timur," I said.

Timur stored his half-chewed cake in one cheek and added, "I'm a visitor."

"This is Lady Lineth," I told him. Bless Lineth. She curtsied, making Timur's face light up. In response, he bowed, his eyes turned anxiously to me as if to ask if he was doing it right. When I nodded, he broke into a smile. "I'm going to the refuge now," I said. "I'll let you know my plans on the way back." He started to turn away, stopped to bow again to Lineth, and galloped back to the egg race, scooping up another cake on the way.

"An interesting visitor," Lineth said. "His clothes looked remarkably like those Beran gave you."

"We might have implied to the dormitory master that

he's visiting you. You don't want more explanation than that, believe me."

"I don't need one because I can already guess at least part of it." She took my arm. "He needed a place to stay. You'll make Beran a fine Wysman one day, Jarka. What is it *The Book of the Wys* says? 'Wysmen and Wyswomen arise in every generation. The faithful know them by their courage and wisdom, and by their selfless care for the weak and the needy.'"

My ears got hot. "If His Highness wants to know how poor folks live, I'm his man." I hitched out the gate and toward the refuge with the lady on my arm, humming happily. I didn't know what was between her and Beran, and truth be told, her illness had set a worry nagging at the back of my head, but she seemed untroubled enough.

Outside the refuge, Lineth pointed out the hollow under the step where the key lived, but she didn't have to. It was the second place I'd have looked, right after the flowerpot. The refuge kids had probably all had it out to play with. Lineth might have led a sheltered life, but Ellyn should have known better. Lineth went inside while I inspected the house front. Having been built against the castle wall limited the possible hiding places. I checked for anyone watching and finally settled on shoving the key behind a loose stone near the ground. I wiped a sweaty palm on my trousers, climbed the step, and entered the refuge.

Lineth was already seated at the table, along with Tally

and all the kids except Rena and Laren. Ellyn was nowhere in sight, and the door to her and Tally's room was closed. The kids all jumped when I came in, one of them knocking a slate to the floor and another shooting to his feet. No doubt about it. The attack on Rena had put them all on edge. They knew too much to ever take safety for granted.

"Sit." Lineth tapped her fingers on the table. "Jarka has things to do, and I'll read you a story so we don't get in his way." Under her stern gaze, they settled a bit, and she started reading from the book of tales I'd loaned Ellyn.

I beckoned Tally outside to show her where the key was. "Remember to tell Ellyn," I said and breathed more easily when she nodded. It wasn't that I was afraid to bring up the key with Ellyn. It would just be better if that discussion happened after I left.

Back inside, Tally sat at the table, and I went toward the row of beds along the back wall, meaning to inspect the area around Rena's for any sign of Rosin having been there. I ran my gaze over the row, trying to pick out the beds Rena had insisted I especially warn the Grabber away from. There were fewer than there had been, I realized. More of the wall showed, the paint nicked by furniture that used to be there and scribbled across with chalk. I'd bet none of the women in charge authorized that, but kids and chalk were here in the same room, so it would take a tower guard on constant duty to keep it from happening. All I found was a lone stocking and three dried up chunks of what it took me a moment to identify as beets. I had to admit the beets made me happy. Wasting food was an offense against the Powers and all that, but I'd eaten my fill in the castle for two months before I passed up a dish of oysters whose slimy texture made me gag. The kid who hid the beets expected someone to feed him the next day.

I saw nothing that pointed to Rosin.

Given the missing Rena and Laren—and Ellyn—it didn't take too much insight to guess where they were. I knocked on the small room's closed door and entered when Ellyn's voice quietly said, "Come."

She was in the rocking chair with Laren in her lap and Rena on one of the two small beds crammed in at the ends of the bigger ones. Laren's eyelids lifted a crack when I entered, but drifted shut again. He looked exhausted. So did Ellyn. Her head drooped back against the chair as if she couldn't hold it up. We stared at one another in silence until I twisted aside and scanned the unmoving Rena. "Has she spoken at all?"

"No."

Rena's hand was icy under my touch when I lifted it gently to look at the bruises circling her wrist. "She couldn't have lain in the keep yard for long or someone would have found her. She was tied up and held for a while. I wonder where."

Ellyn closed her eyes. "I keep asking myself what I could have done. I should have hidden the key better. I shouldn't have gone off to enjoy myself. I should have paid more attention."

I surprised myself by saying, "I'm sorry I picked at you. I know you'd give anything to have stopped what happened to Rena. You couldn't—"

"I could." Her eyes opened, flashing a brown as warm as autumn sun. "My brother died because I wasn't paying attention. He was three years old. Three years! That was the scrap of life he got. I had an excuse then, but I don't now. With Rena, I was as neglectful as my parents always said I was."

"You're *not*. Your parents asked too much of you. *You* ask too much of you."

Shaking her head, she rose, laid Laren in the other small bed, and spread a blanket over him. Then she came close enough that I smelled the harsh soap the refuge used against lice. She spoke low, fingering the knife at her belt. "I'm going to make amends. If I don't, I won't ever be able to live with myself. You're trying to learn who hurt her, and I want to help. Have you looked at Rosin Stonebridge?"

"Rosin?" I tried frantically to think of how to answer. I'd promised Adrya I wouldn't tell anyone Rosin's uncle had killed Ellyn's brother. Had I slipped and mentioned Rosin's name in talking to Ellyn? I didn't think so.

"Yes, Rosin." She waved her hand as if brushing away my slowness. "You know who I mean. Dugan's father. He was here the other morning, looking the kids over, probably picking a victim. And then he was the one who saw us with Rena and shouted for a guard." Her eyes narrowed as she thought about the scene.

"Why do you say 'picking a victim'?"

She wrapped her arms around herself. "This is hard for me to admit because it's about my family." She took a deep breath and planted herself firmly in front of me. "I'd heard the name 'Stonebridge' somewhere before he turned up here, but I couldn't remember where until the middle of last night. And then I woke up knowing I'd overheard my parents whispering it. So as soon as it was light, I went home and asked them." Her voice started to shake. "Rosin's uncle was the one who used sorc—I mean elemental power to steal life from my brother. He did it for Rosin."

"I'm so sorry," I said.

"My parents took money, Jarka! I lived on blood money!" Her jaw was tight but a tear slid down her face. "It's all so wrong."

Without weighing whether it was a good idea, I wrapped her in a one-armed hug. For a moment, her body was stiff, but then she sagged against me. "You weren't much bigger than Rena when your brother was killed."

"And Rena would never let someone hurt Laren." She twisted her fists in my shirt. "I don't know everything a king has to think about, but Thien should have done something and he didn't. So it's up to us."

*It's up to us.* The truth of it slid home. We couldn't rely on Thien's power or anyone else's. We had to use our own. I'd promised Adrya to stay away from Rosin, so I'd stay out of his sight, and I'd speak to him only if he spoke to me and then only to be polite. But I'd find out what happened anyway. "If Rosin is guilty, we'll stop him."

Ellyn's gaze flicked over the bruise on my cheek. "It's not enough to shelter and rock them after they've been hurt."

I pulled back. "I'm not a hurt kid in need of rocking. And a refuge to shelter them is a good thing."

"It is good, and I'd wager anything that you created it because whether you admit it or not, Jarka, there's a hurt kid inside you somewhere still. But this time, I want to stop the hurt before it happens." Her fingers wrapped around her knife hilt again.

"Sweet Powers," I breathed. And meaning to do it even less than I'd meant to hug her, I bent to brush a kiss across her mouth. I jerked back before she had a chance to push me away. The two of us stood there blinking at one another. She touched her lips, then put her hand on the back of my head and pulled my mouth to hers.

"Is Jarka our new uncle now?" a childish voice asked. "Is he going to live here?"

I glanced over my shoulder to see a kid watching us through the half-open door. Then Lineth appeared, guided the kid away, and shut the door.

# Chapter 13

W HEN I STROLLED back into the courtyard, men were lined up along one edge, taking turns kicking their shoes as far as they could get them to fly. A stable hand landed one three quarters of the way across to loud cheers from his co-workers, who'd apparently made up their quarrel. The next man up was Timur.

"You can wash him and dress him, but he still looks like a thug." Dugan said from behind me. I glanced back. He watched Timur, his mouth twisting. Timur kicked, and the boot bounced off the Darklight wheel and splashed into the fountain. Dugan scoffed, and to general hoots, Timur climbed in to wade through the water.

My body still buzzed from having kissed Ellyn, and even more from her kissing me back, so I felt generous enough not to tell Dugan the boot was his. "Aren't you going to join in?" It wasn't like Dugan to pass up a competition and the chance to make himself look good.

"It's kid stuff," Dugan said.

I looked at him more closely. He was leaning against the wall, as if he needed the help to stay on his feet. The spring air was cool, but sun poured gold over everyone in the yard, and yet he was rubbing his own arms as if he was cold. His gaze had drifted from the game to a spot across the yard, and when I followed his line of sight, I saw his parents facing one another in an alcove near the gate to the orchard. Brylla's chin was high, and Rosin actually had his teeth bared. I quickly looked away. Against my will, I cringed for my roommate.

Then I glanced from him to his parents. They were all here, meaning their rooms were empty. If Rena had been tied up and left somewhere, Rosin's rooms were the most likely place. Another kid might be penned up there even now, waiting in terror for Rosin to return. Or maybe there'd be something suggesting where the well was. Maybe that was even what he and Brylla were arguing about. At any rate, I'd never have a better chance to search them. A clog formed in my throat. I'd promised Adrya I wouldn't go near Rosin. He was out here, I reasoned, so whatever I did couldn't upset him and risk his cooperation on the bridge. Besides, I pictured myself telling Ellyn about evidence I'd found there. She'd smile. She might kiss me.

Or not. I shook myself to clear my daydreams.

Timur was still floundering around in the fountain. Getting his attention would mean getting everyone else's too, including Dugan's. I ducked into the nearest castle entry and set off on my own.

I PLACED THE tip of my crutch as quietly as I could and tried to look like I belonged in this corridor along which the guest quarters ranged. A door opened right in front of me, and a very thin man teetered out into the hall, smoothing his shirt as if he were searching for his stomach. I shrank back against the wall to let the man pass. *You see nothing wrong with the boy on the crutch being here,* I silently told the man. *From the streets of Rin to the king's castle, he's at home anywhere.* The man must have had his mind on his next meal because he brushed past without looking at me.

I peeled myself off the wall and realized I'd been reduced to guessing the right door. When a maid came out of a crossing corridor, I stopped her. "Do you know where Lord Rosin's family is staying?"

"Third door on the left." She pointed, then frowned at me. "Are you supposed to be here?"

"Lord Rosin's son is my roommate in the dormitory. He accidentally left these behind when he came to stay with his parents." I held up a pair of blue silk stockings I'd dug out from under Dugan's bed. She must have been convinced I was harmless because she went on her way.

I moved to the door she'd pointed out, darted looks

both ways, and reached for the latch. At the last instant, I drew my hand back, knocked, and waited with the hair on the nape of my neck rising as if it could ward off anyone watching. I waited an eternity, then opened the door, and slipped into the dimly lit room. "Fair day," I croaked. "Dugan?"

The only answer was the hiss of the lamps. I was in a windowless sitting room with doors opening to either side. If Rosin had taken Rena, he'd have had to keep her where his wife and son wouldn't find her. Unless they were in on it, of course, but I couldn't see why they would be. I opened the first door on the left. A gown lay on the bed, waiting for Brylla to come and put it on. There was no men's clothing on the wall hooks though, and no hair pomade on the dresser. Maybe she and Rosin slept apart. I'd heard that nobles did that, though I couldn't fathom the choice. The next door opened on a small room, probably meant for a servant, but currently used by Dugan. I recognized the shirt and trousers crumpled on the floor.

Worried about the time I was taking, I hastened across the sitting room. When I opened the door there and saw the window, I knew I'd found the right room. Trust Rosin to take the best space for himself. I pulled the covers from the curtained bed one by one, then lifted each pillow, scanning for a leather strip that might tie off a braid, a child's stocking, some scrap of Rena. I found nothing. I flung open the two big clothes chests and rooted through them, getting awkwardly down on my knees to do it. Nothing. That didn't mean Rena hadn't been here, of course. Where else would Rosin have taken her?

I blew out my breath and went back into the sitting room. I was moving toward the last side room when the door to the hallway opened, and Brylla entered.

For an instant, she and I gawked at one another. Then she opened her mouth and screamed, "Guards! Guards!"

"You don't have to do that," I said. "I was just leaving. I was looking for Dugan." I took a step toward her.

She backed into the hallway. "Guards!"

Booted feet pounded down the hall, and two Tower Guards ran around Brylla into the sitting room.

"Why is he here? He doesn't belong here." Brylla was on the edge of hysteria and maybe slightly over it. I must have been scarier than I realized.

"I was looking for Dugan," I told a guard. "I knocked, and I thought I heard him say come in, so I did. These are his." I yanked the stockings out of my belt.

"He's thieving." Brylla snatched the stockings out of my hand.

"Go ahead and search me." I extended my free arm. I knew the routine, and this time, I really *was* innocent. Of thieving, anyway.

The two guards closed in. One turned my pockets inside out and showed Brylla what he found—a stub of chalk, a used handkerchief, a fluff of lint—while the other efficiently ran his hands over my body, even probing into my shoes.

I watched Brylla from the corner of my eye, so as not to scare her further. She stood breathing heavily, her back to the wall. She barely glanced at the contents of my pockets before she shook her head. "I want the king to know about this," she said. "I want this boy warned to stay away from me."

"That's not necessary, really," I said hastily. "From now on, Dugan can come and get anything he forgot."

"I want to talk to Thien myself." Brylla glared at the guards. "He and my husband have an agreement. I will not have this street boy poking through my belongings."

The two guards exchanged a look. One of them sighed. "Come along, boy. Let's see what His Majesty thinks about this."

I dragged myself out into the hallway, a guard on each side as if they thought I might hotfoot it away. Brylla sailed ahead of us, chin high.

"What did you do to her?" one of the guards murmured.

"Nothing. I don't know why she's so spooked."

The guards guided me along the hall, down the stairs, and through the corridors to Thien's council chamber, where another guard stood near the door. "Is His Majesty within?" asked one of my guards.

"He's with Adrya," the door guard said.

Stone it. Adrya wouldn't be happy even if I hadn't gone near Rosin himself. For the first time, I seriously feared being bounced out of the castle before sunset.

"Tell the king Lady Brylla wishes to complain about Adrya's apprentice. She says he broke into the Stonebridges' rooms."

The door guard ducked inside and came out again almost immediately. "You can go in."

Brylla went first. The guards holding me nudged me into the room. Adrya and Thien looked up from their seats at the table filling most of the small space. We all bowed. No one had trimmed the lamp since the last council meeting, and I blinked at the sting of smoke.

Thien's eyelids drooped, half-shuttering his keen eyes. He nodded to the guards. "You may go." They closed the door behind them, and for a moment, the room was silent. In my role as Adrya's apprentice, I'd sat through many meetings in this room. I knew better than to speak until Thien gave me permission. Adrya's glare bored into my head as I waited. Then Thien nodded to Brylla. "You wished to speak to me, lady?"

"This...this street thief was in our apartments, Your Majesty. He touched our things." She shuddered. My ears grew warm at the horror in her voice. "Who knows what he stole."

Thien inclined his head toward me. "If you have an explanation, you may give it."

"I was looking for Dugan, sir. He's my roommate and he left something in our room that I thought he might want. I saw the lady and Lord Rosin in the yard, so I didn't think I'd bother them." I forced the words around the heart that had climbed from my chest into my throat.

"He shouldn't have been there," Brylla broke in, then pinched her lips when Thien raised an eyebrow at her.

We all waited in silence that felt heavy as a loaded cart. Finally, Thien said, "Jarka, I forbid you to go near *any* of the Stonebridges."

"Yes, sir," I said, keeping my voice neutral. I saw Adrya's nostrils flare. She was probably dying to remind me and inform the king she'd already told me to keep away from Rosin.

"You hear him, Lady Brylla," Thien said. "If you're content to place your trust in my authority, you may go."

Gripping the back of one of the empty council chairs, Brylla stayed where she was, as if she doubted the power of Thien's order. I looked at a scuff mark on the floor to hide my astonishment. "Sir," she said, "there is another matter. My husband was supposed to have spoken to you about this, but you haven't yet granted him a meeting."

Thien ran his hand over his face. "Yes?"

"It's private, sir." Brylla wrinkled her nose in my direction.

"My apprentice has never repeated anything he learned in the council chamber." Adrya sounded offended, which made me feel a bit more kindly toward her. She pointed to my usual place on a bench under a wall map of Rinland. I was relieved to make myself a smaller target by backing out of Thien's line of vision and collapsing.

Brylla's hands unknotted from the back of the chair and began twisting together. "As you know, sir, my son Dugan has been under your care for four years now."

I sat up straight, torn between wanting to know everything about my roommate and feeling wrong for nosing into another boy's life.

"He's grown into a young man who, I hope, pleases you." She waited for Thien to nod, then said, "He tells me he's fallen in love and wants permission to marry."

My breath sped up. Surely Dugan didn't fancy himself in love with Ellyn?

"He's young to marry," Thien observed mildly.

"He is." Brylla drew a deep breath. "But he's old enough to be sure of his feelings for Lady Lineth."

For an instant, I thought I must have misheard.

Thien glanced toward the map over my head then back at Brylla. "That's out of the question." He folded his hands before him on the table. "Lady Lineth is already promised elsewhere." My heart pounded. Thien must have decided to let Beran marry Lineth after all.

Brylla's shoulders sagged. "I was told she and His Highness—"

"Her intended isn't His Highness," Thien said.

"Then who?" Brylla snapped her mouth shut, too late to catch the question. I leaned toward Thien, as eager as she was to hear the answer, and probably just as dismayed.

"You will forgive me for keeping my plans to myself," Thien said dryly. "You may go, lady."

Brylla stayed still for only an instant before curtsying and groping her way out of the room as if Thien had struck her blind.

When the door closed behind her, Adrya said, "That's about money. As I told you, Rosin has run through the fortune Brylla brought him."

Thien rubbed his jaw. "My main concern is that bridge." He looked at the map again. "I can't allow the Stonebridges to ally themselves with anyone. Lineth's family is already smarting under her father's disgrace. If she marries Dugan, they might feel he gave them someplace else to put their loyalties."

Adrya shrugged. "The match with Lord Nithron's son is better for us anyway."

"So you pointed out when you suggested it," Thien said.

I pawed through my memory of council meetings for some clue to who Lord Nithron was and finally came up with a minor landholder in Longrass Province.

"That fool Rosin is a constant problem," Thien murmured. He lowered his gaze to land on me. "Adrya tells me you have accused Lord Rosin of harming the girl found in the courtyard."

Well, stone Adrya. I hauled myself to my feet and drew myself as tall as I could. "Yes, sir. I think he hurt her the same way his uncle once hurt a boy."

"I told you he's unlikely to have done that," Adrya put in.

"Have you proof, Jarka?" Thien asked.

"No, sir. Not yet. He did go to the refuge and eye the children though."

Thien's mouth pursed. "The child was from the refuge Lady Lineth runs? I was told the refuge children attacked others at the puppet show yesterday. Given that Lady Lineth will be leaving for Longrass as soon as Darklight is over, perhaps you and she should begin closing the place."

Ice clogged my throat. "Please don't do that, sir. Please find some way to keep it open even if Lady Lineth leaves. She'd put up money, I know."

"Her new husband would have the final say about that," Thien said. "We'll leave it for now. However, I expect you to do what I say."

I braced myself. A bargain was being struck, but Thien didn't really have to rely on bargains, and he was issuing an order that he expected to be obeyed.

"Lord Rosin knows better than to violate my hospitality by harming a child in the castle, in the city of Rin, or anywhere in my kingdom," Thien said. "That being so, I charge you to cease spreading accusations for which you have no proof, and which damage our peace. After prayers tomorrow, we will warn people to guard their children well, without naming anyone of course."

I stared straight ahead. Every muscle in my body was seized with the insane impulse to spring into action, to grab my king and squeeze until I forced him to do what I wanted. That edge in Thien's voice made me think he

knew Rosin had misused water's power. Given the fate of
Ellyn's brother, of course he did. He knew there'd been
evil worked, yet he was going to do nothing about it. I'd
known that, but seeing it in action was far worse. "Sir,
what about justice for Rena? Someone hurt her in ways the
healer doesn't even understand, ways that sound twisted.
Whoever did it should be punished."

"One of the guards is looking into the matter." Thien
put his fingertips together and leaned forward. "Jarka, I
have you in the castle because my son wishes it and
because Adrya believes you have the potential to be a
Wysman, for Beran, if not for me. But I warn you now and
only this once. If you disrupt my rule, I will send you so
far away, you'll need a map to find the stars."

Unable to move, I stared into Thien's set face. Silence
swelled against the ceiling and walls. Then Thien leaned
back in his chair. "Adrya, I thank you for your counsel.
You and Jarka may go."

Adrya pushed back her chair, bowed, and touched my
arm to herd me out of the room.

ADRYA HUSTLED ME a short distance away from the door
guard and spoke with a lowered voice. "Where's your
wind box?"

I met her gaze levelly. "I don't have it."

She scoffed. "Shall we go and search your room?"

"If you want to." We started walking. "Does Lineth know about this betrothal?"

"Not yet, though surely she's expecting something like it. She obviously can't stay here. The match with Nithron's son is a good one for her, all things considered, and her fortune should make Nithron grateful to the king, but not so powerful that he becomes a threat to Thien or his own lord. As a matter of fact, a stronger Nithron will balance things there a little better. What's more, the girl's attractive, which should also please Nithron's son. It's a happy solution all the way around."

"No, it's not. Not for Lineth and not for Beran either. When are you going to tell him?"

Adrya shrugged. "When he comes back. I assume he's expecting something like this too."

"This marriage has been all agreed on, and you didn't even tell Beran? If he just walks away from Lineth, he's as big a fool as Thien is."

"Mind your mouth," Adrya said sharply. "You think this doesn't cost the king? Choosing between his son's happiness and the peace of his kingdom?"

I didn't care about any 'cost' to Thien. I felt sick—sick at what was about to happen to Lineth, sick at the way Thien was willing to sacrifice poor kids to keep his nobles in line. "Lineth's pretty, that's true. But she didn't make her own face or body the way she makes herself generous and brave. She'd be good for Rinland when Beran becomes king. She understands people, and she feels for them."

"Do you want to be a Wysman or not?" Adrya demanded. "If so, you'll have to make hard choices of your own. You can spend time running around the city saving one person here, another there. Or you can be in a position to advise a king to make life better for the country as a whole."

"After what I just saw in the council chamber, maybe I don't want to advise a king. What kind of adviser would I be if I let kids be hurt so I could get a piece of a king's power?" I found I didn't care if it sounded like I was accusing her.

"Don't play the fool. I know you too well," she said. I opened my mouth, but she stopped me, saying, "Lineth's betrothal is done. That's the last I want to hear from you about it."

I flung my crutch so far in front of me, I nearly fell. "Then what about Rosin?" I cast around desperately for some course of action. "I understand you don't want to upset Rosin because of the bridge, but if you show me how to get into the secret passages, maybe I can find proof of what he's doing and save some poor kid. If I don't, he'll never know, and his bridge will still be safe." We entered the dormitory corridor.

"Jarka, the king just told you to leave the Stonebridges alone. Are you planning to cross him?"

"No! And I don't want to make an enemy of Rosin if he's innocent. You're sure he is, right? So finding out the truth won't hurt anyone. Unless, of course, it's Rosin you're worried about."

"Let it go."

I led her to my room. She scanned the small space, wrinkling her nose. I sniffed and registered the smell of dirty stockings and sweat and boys that I normally didn't notice. "Have a look around," I said and then suddenly remembered the book under my mattress. I borrowed books all the time, but the fact that this one was hidden would make her take a good hard look at it. And when she did, she'd recognize it as the one she said wasn't for me. She wouldn't even have to open it, just glimpse the stone bridge on the cover. One part of me didn't care. Let her and Thien kick me out. But the biggest part of me couldn't let that happen until I brought Rosin down.

Frantically rehearsing excuses, I watched her go through my belongings, then drop to her knees and look under both beds. She sat back on her heels and looked up at me. "Where did you put it?"

"Put what?" I echoed stupidly.

"What do you think? Your wind box."

I clamped my mouth shut.

She pushed to her feet. "What are you planning to do with it?"

"Nothing, I swear. If I had it. Which I don't. And if I did, it would be because it's mine."

She looked at me from under half-lowered lids. "If I see or hear about you using it, I promise you will be sorry." She marched out of the room.

I blinked at the still-swinging curtain. She knew I had the wind box. She had to know, and yet she'd let it go. How unexpectedly forgiving of her.

I waited until I heard the door close behind her, then braced one hand on my bed and leaned over to look. The book was gone. I collapsed to sit on my bed, staring blankly at the wall across the room. What had happened here? Someone hid the book in a place that implicated me, but then they took it away again. Did they need it? A chill slipped inside my collar. If their channeling of water had gone wrong the first time, yes, they did. Then my eyes snapped into focus, looking straight at the runes carved into the stone wall. "Seek the true way," the same words that were on the panel leading to the secret passage in the library. I found myself on my feet, across the room, touching the runes. What if the secret passages had more than one entrance?

# Chapter 14

I RAN MY fingers over the carved runes. Power rippled under my touch, faint but there, like the throb of Mother Earth's heart. I realized this must be how the Stonebridges' book had arrived and left. Rosin was using the passages.

I put my palm over the word 'way' and pushed. Nothing happened. I started with 'seek' and pushed each one in turn. Nothing. I said the words out loud, then pushed on each one as I named it. The wall stayed where it was.

I stepped back and contemplated the place where I thought the door would be. When Adrya had emerged into the library, the panel had swung into the room, not out to the passage. Maybe I'd been pushing when I should have pulled. I hooked my fingertips into the shallow incisions and tried to pull, but no matter how hard I tried to wedge them, my fingers slid free, and I succeeded only in tearing the nail on my index finger. Cursing, I shook my hand. This was pointless. If I was supposed to pull, the runes had worn too smooth for me to get hold of them. I blew out a breath. Maybe I was wrong. Maybe this was just a stone wall, and I was a fool. But surely I hadn't mistaken that tingle of power living in the words carved here long ago. I *must* have missed something. I ran my hand down the trail of words, murmuring their message. With a soft squeak, a section of the wall swung toward me. I shuffled hastily out of the way, then stood gaping at the space that had lain there quietly for the entire time I slept in this room.

When the door reached the end of its swing and began to close, I lunged into the shrinking opening, then teetered to a halt on the room-side edge, my free hand straining to hold the door open. The passage was soot dark. I let the door thud shut, limped back across the room, and seized a candle from the shelf. I had my hand on the edge of the curtain, meaning to light it at the hearth in the hallway, when I heard the dormitory master. "I want all these curtain rings replaced. I swear the boys swing on them."

I froze. I could hardly light a candle in front of the master in the middle of the day and not have him ask where I expected to use it. Explore in the dark or wait for a better time? I ran my hand over the runes. Exploring in the dark felt like what I'd been doing so far. Might as well keep it up. The secret door opened, and I plunged through. The door swung back into place, and I stood in darkness as thick as if I'd been closed in a coffin. I'd better be able to get out again. I groped to be sure there were runes on this side, then yanked my hand away when I heard the jingle of curtain rings. I pictured the look on anyone who saw me tumble out. Stowing the candle in my pocket, I set off, my free hand trailing along the wall.

I'd gone only a short distance before my fingers slid into nothingness and a draft told me I'd reached a crossway. When I turned my head left, I saw a thin shaft of light slanting across the passage. I limped that way, to find it streaming through a hole in the wall no bigger than my fingertip. I put my eye to it and saw the dormitory master, seated at his desk, running his finger over what looked like an account book. I pulled back and stood for a moment, trying to picture the various castle rooms and hallways and the way they fit together. The castle's unpredictable twists and turns made a lot more sense now. Assuming all the passages connected, if I kept going this way and found a stairway down, I'd be near the library, the only other entrance I was sure of. More important, I wouldn't be far from the guest quarters, and if his room had a similar peephole, I could observe Rosin when he didn't know anyone was there.

Leaving the tiny light from the master's room behind, I tried to follow the map in my head. A faint breeze drifted over my face. The feel of it made me uneasy. It was laden with the same elemental disturbance I'd felt in the yard when the fountain blew up. Just when I began to wonder if

I was wandering in circles, I jammed my toe into something, and toppled nose first, bashing my knee against a rock-hard edge. My crutch clattered to the floor. Stars exploded in the dark.

I rocked, clutching my knee and blinking back tears until the phantom sticking hot pins in my knee backed off. I drew a long breath and groped to find what had tripped me. My hand slid off a shallow raised ledge, then plunged to a second, lower level. I'd found the stairs going down and was lucky I hadn't cartwheeled all the way to the second floor. Crutch back in hand, I dragged myself erect and lowered myself to the first step. My foot barely fit. A trickle of sweat ran down my backbone. I crept steeply downward in a space barely shoulder wide. When my foot finally slid onto a level space, my leg nearly gave way with relief. Not only was I on a solid floor again, but ahead of me, another narrow beam of light pricked through a spy hole and split the darkness.

I sniffed. The air in the tunnel smelled faintly of a mix of lamp oil and Adrya's rose perfume, meaning she'd been in here recently. I needed to keep my ears perked for warning of her approach. When I put my eye to the spy hole, I found only an empty guest room. The passage I was in turned sharply into a dark length pierced by more spy holes. The next one showed me a woman whose maid was dressing her hair. I eyed the woman's shift-clad body, decided I was being creepy, and moved along.

Ahead, I heard a familiar woman's voice, raised and

shrill, catching every bit of my attention. I pressed my eye to the next spy hole, and sure enough, in their sitting room, Brylla and Rosin were continuing the war they'd been having in the yard.

"I told you you should have talked to Thien about Dugan and Lineth sooner." Brylla paced across the room, then spun back so her skirts swirled around her in a tornado of fury. "Now it's too late. For the second—no, *third* time, you've ruined us."

Rosin sat in the padded armchair, leaning forward with his elbows on his knees and his face in his hands. "It was the payment to the boy's family that ruined us. That wasn't my fault."

"Oh no, of course not," she sneered.

"It wasn't! And now that lame boy is accusing me."

"I thought you got Adrya to call him off."

"I did, but your finding him in our rooms suggests he's still at it. If he doesn't back down, I don't know what I'll do. Thien will execute me."

"You are the whiniest man I have ever met. When has Thien ever made a single move against you? And Adrya is a bitch. She probably did nothing. You should have seen her looking down her nose at me in that meeting." She stopped pacing and contemplated him with her eyes narrowed and her hands on her hips. "I've seen you flirting with every unmarried noble woman. You think you'll save yourself by divorcing me and snaring one of them. You know I won't go back to my father without a fight, don't you?"

Rosin sat bolt upright. "What makes you think I have that in mind? And you'll do what I tell you."

"We'll see." She stormed from the room.

Rosin stared at the door that had slammed shut behind her, then went to the corner table, poured himself a cup of wine, and drained it. Then he followed his wife out of the room.

I backed away. What horrible people. They didn't care who they hurt and were just floundering around trying to save themselves. And Rosin was aware I was hunting him. Given how ruthless the man was, that meant it was time to find Timur.

I made my way back along the passage. Once I'd passed the last spy hole, I slowed down and tested each step so I wouldn't stumble into the stairway. Things weren't quite where I expected them to be, and I had to grope along the wall for a while before I found a flight, though it was a different set of stairs because it led down rather than up. I was only on the second floor, so down might also mean out. I was in too much of a hurry to be careful and slipped twice before I decided to sit and bump down on my rear. At the bottom, I climbed to my feet and headed off again. The hand I was keeping on the wall slid over a crack in the stones, and I nearly went on before I realized what I'd felt and fumbled for it again. When my fingers found it, I traced it carefully. Not a crack. A rune. I felt for those over and under it, then swept my hand down the lot. "Seek the true way."

A section of the wall swung away from me, and I scrambled out into late afternoon sun bright enough to make my eyes water after so long in the dark. I was in a sheltered gap behind a flight of stairs. The ones leading to the walkway in the old keep, I realized, and a chill settled in my gut. This was the spot where Ellyn found Rena.

Only a handful of people lingered in the main yard, which meant it was almost supper time and Timur would be in the Great Hall.

In the washroom outside the Hall, I found my palms black with whatever dirt had been on the passageway walls. I washed hastily and limped into the Hall, where the meal was indeed already underway. I sidled along behind the benches until I reached my place next to Adrya.

She glared at me. "I'd about decided you didn't mean to eat. You're not sulking over Thien's orders, are you?"

"No." I dropped down onto the bench and reached for the platter of roast beef and onions set between my trencher and Adrya's.

"Good. And not that I doubt you, but I asked the guard captain to put a man on the dormitory door tonight. None of you boys should be roaming around after dark. Nothing good can come of that."

I snapped around to glare at her. "What?"

"You were in the library last night after curfew. Did you think I didn't notice?"

"You don't trust me even to get a book?"

"I was young myself once, Jarka. I know what it's like. Now settle down and eat."

Not having much choice, I did as I was told. As I ate, I stole a look at Thien, but the king was, of course, paying me no attention, despite having threatened to ship me to the end of the earth, a threat that apparently stuck in my mind much more firmly than it lodged in his. Thien had the lord of Longrass Province seated at his elbow, and the two of them were engrossed in conversation, maybe about Lineth's marriage. I didn't see her anywhere in the Hall. I considered breaking my pledge to keep council chamber matters secret and tell her about the marriage. I'd been surprised and pleased by Adrya's defending my discretion to Brylla though. What's more, I wasn't sure knowing about the marriage would do Lineth any good. It sounded as if the matter was settled.

I turned to scan the lower ends of the table, and found Timur seated with some boys I didn't know, probably servants who'd come with the visitors. Or rather, Timur was seated near them. They'd slid along the benches to leave a wide space on either side of him. Timur was shoveling meat into his mouth as if he hadn't eaten it in a month, which he probably hadn't, but he evidently felt my eyes on him because he met my gaze and waved before falling on his food again.

I swung my gaze back to the upper end of the table where Rosin sat with Brylla and Dugan. I watched them over the edge of my ale cup almost unable to believe they were the same people I'd seen ripping one another's guts out in their rooms. Brylla laughed and looked through her lashes at the young lord on her left, while Dugan sulked between her and his father. Rosin looked jolliest of the three, clapping for the minstrel, offering bites of pastry to the woman on his right. Maybe I'd get lucky and he'd occupy himself with her tonight and leave kids alone.

*Enjoy yourself now.* I set the cup down and drove the point of my knife into a hunk of beef. *Tomorrow, I'm coming for you. Whatever it takes.*

"Stop looking so fierce," Adrya said. "You're in the king's Hall, not a city alley."

*Since there's not much difference, I don't care.*

# Chapter 15

THE NEXT MORNING, I was lighting the brazier when Thien and Adrya entered the Great Hall. Hastily, I backed to the rear of the platform, the box of sulfur sticks still in my hand. I tucked it into my pocket, then waited while Adrya burned the incense, tapping my crutch against the floor. She frowned over her shoulder, and I tightened my muscles to keep myself still. In the night, I'd worried about how Rena was faring and even more about whether Rosin was hunting for a new kid. Time was running short for him as well as for me. From now on, I vowed, I'd keep my distance, but I wouldn't let him out of my sight.

The crowd finally grew still enough to suit Adrya. As she opened *The Book*, I thought I saw something pale flutter out from between the pages. I narrowed my eyes. Gleaming in a shaft of light from the high windows, a white thread drifted toward the floor but at the last moment caught on the hem of Adrya's dark skirt. I looked up to find Adrya staring at the open book wide-eyed, as if somehow it had surprised her. As surely as if I'd seen her do it, I knew what had happened. She'd laid a thread between the pages she wanted to read that morning. It had fallen out, and now she was confronted with a passage she wasn't prepared to speak about. I didn't know whether to laugh at her dismay or be shocked by what a cheat the woman was. I'd known she shaped her interpretations sometimes, but not that she thwarted the Powers' choice of the passage to be read. I had to admire her nerve. If I were her, I'd be constantly watching the sky for lightning bolts.

Adrya read at a crawling pace. Stalling for time, I judged. "'To each man and woman, a number of days is given. We live in joy and sorrow, pleasure and pain, before we are gathered to our rest in the arms of Mother Earth. Time is a river that never flows backward. We pass life to our children. Only those with hearts of stone would wish to keep it for themselves instead.'"

I shifted my weight from foot to crutch and back. Adrya might have trouble interpreting the truth of that passage, but it fit my fears about Rosin like the sheath on Ellyn's belt fit her knife.

Adrya cleared her throat. "How perfect are the words of *The Book* for the Feast of Darklight. The young do depend on us, their elders, to shape a world in which they can live in peace and plenty." Adrya's voice steadied as she found her way from what she'd read to something worth saying. She swept her gaze over the nobles summoned to Rin to renew their fealty pledges. "Only the stonehearted would chance pushing a country into war to increase their own gain. We are fortunate to have a ruler who would never allow that to happen." It wasn't up to Adrya's usual polished standards, but it wasn't bad for something made up on the spot, and I had to admit, that reference to "stonehearted" sounded like a warning to Rosin. "May the Powers bless us all," Adrya said, signaling the end of prayers.

Eager to be on the hunt, I waited for Thien to leave, but instead the king gestured to his steward, who climbed up on the platform as Adrya backed away to give him room. The crowd stirred. They knew what was coming even if I didn't.

"Gentle people of Rinland," the steward said, "before anything else, I want to tell those of you who haven't heard that a hurt child was left in the castle courtyard two days ago. Please watch your children with care until we know what happened." The crowd murmured as people who didn't know about Rena demanded the news from those who did. I could swear I heard someone say "The Grabber."

I studied the Stonebridges in their usual place at the front of the crowd. All three of them stared straight ahead, faces expressionless.

The steward waited for quiet, then spoke again. "I'm

told that the Sharing Wheel is now ready for any young man who wants to try for the prize. Young sirs, you have a chance to win gold or health and long life, and in the attempt, you're sure to entertain the rest of us." Laughter and a few cheers rippled across the relieved crowd. "We have new cider and aged cheese," the steward went on. "I invite you to break your fast in the courtyard." He jumped off the platform into the crowd, which was already flowing out the double doorway, even though the king wasn't quite out of the room.

Adrya clapped *The Book of the Wys* shut. "Did you touch this?" she asked.

"Of course not. You've had it with you, haven't you?"

Staring at *The Book*, Adrya chewed her lip. Then she gave her shoulders a shake. "Enjoy the holiday." She gathered the book, a little gingerly I thought, and followed Thien.

I swung myself down off the platform and went after Rosin, who was moving with the departing crowd. I lost him in the crush through the doorway, but emerged into the courtyard, scanned until I spotted him standing with Brylla and Dugan, and only then followed the smell of fresh bread to the tables outside the kitchens. A scullion offered me a mug of cider, and a slab of thickly buttered bread topped with cheese. I managed to grab the bread in my crutch hand and the mug in the other and moved out of the way, keeping an eye on Rosin.

A Darklight wheel spun in the fountain, and next to it,

folks gathered around a long trough that looked a lot like the ones I'd seen on previous holidays in New Square. A second water wheel was set in it so that the wheel's wide paddles ran from one end of the trough to the other. It spun with the fall of water from a chute jammed between it and the fountain. Over the far end of the trough, a small leather bag hung from a hook. At the near end, I spotted Gelas among several young men shedding their boots, preparing to try to walk the length of the wheel and seize the little bag of coins. Around them, onlookers laughed and jeered.

"Ready for a cold bath?" one man called.

The young men grinned. One of them shot a shy look at a pretty girl, who nodded encouragingly.

Rosin prodded Dugan, who shook his head. Studying him, I wasn't surprised. Dugan still looked ill. The morning sun showed patches of scarlet on his cheekbones. Eyes on the ground, he edged a little away from his parents. For the second time in two days, I felt sorry for him. Apparently deciding he'd given his daily ration of fatherly encouragement, Rosin swiveled to eye a pretty woman near the fountain.

Brylla turned her head away and strolled stiffly in my general direction, though it wasn't me she was after. Instead, she watched Lady Lineth who had come up next to me, smiling and shaking her head at the water wheel. "At least it's a warm morning." She took a tiny bite from the piece of dry bread she held. Brylla halted, evidently unwilling to come close to me, even if Lineth was there.

The news of Lineth's betrothal swelled up to fill my head, threatening to spill out of my mouth, but she looked so happy I hated to spoil her peace. This must be one of the hard choices Adrya claimed Wysones had to make. I sipped my cider, then pinched my crutch in my armpit and hunched over to reach my bread and cheese.

"Let me hold that." Lineth took the cider cup from my hand, all the while watching the steward explain the rules to the wheel walkers.

I chewed hard on my bread. Thien had a lot to answer for.

From near the kitchens, Timur hurried toward us. I had to admit Dugan was right about one thing: Timur was skinny and half-a-head shorter than I was, but he did look like a thug, even in my clothes. His bruised face didn't help, but the impression was mostly a matter of the way he glared at anyone who dared to even squint in his direction. I understood. Timur's life had taught him to warn off trouble before it came too close. He halted next to us and nodded a greeting.

"It's Timur, isn't it?" Lineth said. "Are you having a good visit?"

He nodded so hard that a strand of hair came loose from its tail.

Lineth smiled. "You'll be sorry to go home then."

Timur's face stiffened. "I'm never doing that."

I wished that could be true, but it was more likely I'd

be joining him on the streets.

Lineth eyed him thoughtfully, but all our attentions were drawn by the cries rising from near the fountain as a castle guard became the first to try to walk the wheel. He stepped off the platform and jigged along the wheel, lifting his knees high over the sweeping paddles, but he went only a few yards before the wheel got ahead of him and he plunged into the trough. He bobbed up at once, spluttering and sweeping wet tails of hair from his face. The other guards in the crowd hooted and laughed. The one in the trough shared the laugh good-naturedly and climbed out.

"See the purse at the other end of the wheel?" Lineth asked Timur. "It holds gold coins that the king put up as the prize. The first one to cross the wheel wins it, but then he has to decide if he wants to keep it or give it away. If he gives it away, the Powers bless him with health and long life." She grinned. "Usually the winner gives the prize to his sweetheart if he has one. That way he hopes to both give it away and keep it."

Timur opened his mouth to speak, and I interrupted. It was probably best if Timur talked as little as possible. "The king also puts up the prize for the wheel in New Square, so townsmen can impress their sweethearts too." Not that I'd ever dreamed of trying to walk the wheel to impress a girl. I didn't see the girl I'd like to impress in the courtyard anyway.

And then without warning there she was, standing at

Lineth's other side. My mouth tingled with the memory of kissing her, and I felt myself grinning like a loon. "Fair morning, lady," she said, speaking to Lineth but looking sideways at me. It seemed to me her mouth was trying to smile too.

"Fair morning, Ellyn," Lineth said. "Have you met Timur?"

Ellyn's brows drew together. "Maybe." I could almost feel her effort to remember where she'd seen Timur before. She blinked when he bowed, that undoubtedly not being part of her previous experience with him.

"I'm a visitor," Timur said.

"How's Rena?" I asked hastily.

"The same." She held up a bottle. "I'm fetching more medicine from the healer, but it doesn't seem to be doing any good. Are you giving lessons today?" she asked Lineth.

"No. Truthfully, I'm not feeling well and think I'd do best just to go back to my room. Would you like to come with me, Jarka? I was hoping you could ask the wind when Beran will be home." Her voice was steady, but her pale cheeks went pink.

I looked across the yard at Rosin. "I can't, lady. Not now."

Her shoulders drooped. "That's all right. I know you have duties."

Aware of Ellyn glaring at me, I added, "Maybe later."

"If you can, I'd appreciate it." Lineth handed me back my cider and went into the castle.

Ellyn moved close enough to speak so only I would hear. Her breath tickled my bruised ear. "Jarka, she needs news of Beran. Really *needs* it. Can you not spare the bit of time it would take to help her?"

"I can't. I'm worried about Lineth too. Truly I am. But I can't leave Rosin alone right now."

Ellyn looked across the yard at him and fingered her knife. "Of course you're right. It's just…"

"I know," I said. "I'm only guessing." We shared a sober look.

Timur nudged me and poked his chin toward the water wheel where Gelas was just venturing off the platform. He took exactly two steps before tumbling off the wheel with a splash that made watchers skip out of the way. He popped up, glaring through the water sheeting down his face.

Timur's mouth curved. He walked toward the wheel.

I grabbed for his sleeve too late and muffled a groan. Before we left the dormitory that morning, I should have reminded Timur to keep his head down. Otherwise, sooner or later, someone like Ellyn who'd seen him in New Square might recognize him.

Timur walked through the group of young men arguing over who was next and vaulted up onto the platform without even taking off Dugan's boots. "Here," one man said, but Timur had already stepped out onto the wheel. With his arms stretched out like wings, he ran down the length of the wheel and snatched the prize before the echo of the protest had finished bouncing off the castle walls. He jumped to the flagstones and pressed the purse to his chest, elbows out as if to ward off thieves.

For an instant, no one spoke. Then the steward cried, "We have a winner!" The onlookers applauded weakly. "Do you want to keep the purse," the steward asked Timur, "or do you want to give it to someone else and earn the Powers' blessing?" The steward swept his hand over the crowd.

"Don't be daft." Timur tucked the purse into his pocket and trotted back toward me and Ellyn, leaving the steward with his mouth hanging open. I couldn't help laughing.

"Well done," Ellyn said when Timur halted beside us. Across the courtyard, Dugan glared from Timur to me to Ellyn and ran his tongue over his cracked lips.

The crowd in the courtyard began to drift apart. I was trying to keep an eye on Rosin when one of Thien's pages caught my arm. "Jarka, a gate guard said to tell you your cousin came and wanted to talk to you. The guard told her to wait."

"Is she all right?" I asked.

"He didn't say." The page skipped off leaving me with the sense that I'd acted out this same scene two days ago and ended up with my face bloody and Lyssa telling me to stay away.

"Do you have to go to your cousin, Jarka?" Ellyn asked. "If you do, I can watch Rosin."

"You can't in the castle." *Or in the passages*, though I couldn't tell her about them. I spotted Rosin passing through a doorway. Curse Lyssa anyway. Adrya was right. If Lyssa wouldn't listen to me, there wasn't much I could do. She wanted me to stay away, so I would. I'd send Timur to track Rosin in the hallways, while I went back into the secret passages to see what I could learn without alarming him and putting Thien's precious bridge in danger.

"Fair morning, Ellyn," said an unwelcome voice. I turned to find Dugan looming over me, blocking me from going after his father. "Are these two bothering you?" He jerked his head at me and Timur.

"Not at all," Ellyn said coolly. "I was just on my way to the infirmary. Send word if you need me, Jarka." She patted my arm, making me freeze for an instant, then swept past Dugan and into the infirmary wing.

I started to follow, but Dugan planted his hand on my chest and curled his lip at Timur. Abruptly, he staggered hard enough that I grabbed his elbow to steady him. Sweat shone on his forehead.

"Are you all right?" I asked.

He shook me off and spoke to Timur. "You're not a visitor. That's a lie, isn't it?" He jerked his head toward me again. "You're one of his filthy friends."

"This is none of your business, Dugan," I said.

"I was talking to him, not you."

Timur bared his teeth.

I sidled between them. "You're after him because of me, though. You going to start a fight in the king's courtyard?"

Dugan smiled unpleasantly. "I don't have to."

Over his shoulder, I saw Gelas approaching, dripping from his unexpected swim but buckling his sword belt. His eyes flicked between me and Timur, but he spoke to Dugan. "What have you learned, sir?"

Sir?

"Nothing yet," Dugan said. "Why don't we all take a walk—or in the cripple's case, gimp—into the old keep?"

"Sure thing." Timur immediately started toward the gate leading to the older courtyard. Gelas hurried after him, and Dugan grabbed my arm, forcing me to follow with him shuffling along beside me, still pale and sweating. I didn't have time for this.

We'd just reached the gate when Brylla called, "Dugan! Come with me, Dugan."

I turned to see her beckoning, for once aware of her son getting into trouble.

"Wait," Dugan said to Gelas. "I'll be back." He walked toward his mother.

"Go." I shoved Timur through the gate.

Gelas grabbed for my arm, but I swept his feet out from under him with my crutch. He went down hard on the flagstones.

I scrambled after Timur, flinging the tip of my crutch far ahead and hopping to keep up with it.

"Where to?" Timur stopped and looked around the yard. Not a soul was in sight.

For once, I knew where I was going—the place I'd intended to be all along. I urged Timur out of sight in the gap behind the staircase. Then, as Timur gaped, I ran my finger down the runes and spoke the words. The wall swung toward us. I grabbed Timur's arm and dragged him into the black space beyond. Behind us, the door swung shut.

# Chapter 16

TIMUR'S FINGERS SPASMED around my forearm. "It's black as a crow's insides in here. Where are we?"

I opened my mouth and then closed it. "I can't tell you. Look around and guess."

"It's too dark to look. Open the door."

"Don't like the dark?" I was annoyed enough at having lost Rosin to feel nasty amusement over Timur the Thug quaking in the dark.

He let go of my arm. For a long moment, he was silent. "My granny locked me in the root cellar for three days once," he said tonelessly.

I flinched. "There are other ways out. Come on. Feel along that wall for a hallway or a stairwell." I groped along the left-hand wall. Yesterday's adventure had taught me I had no idea how these passages fit together, but obviously there were other doorways. We just had to find one with nobody on the other side. Timur's breathing rasped more and more desperately.

"Light!" He veered off into a passage on the right.

"Hush."

A thin shaft of light slanted across the velvet dark. Timur laid his face against the wall next to it. "Open it," he whispered.

I ran my hand along the wall but found no runes. "It's not a doorway." I set my eye to the spy hole and found myself looking into Thien's small audience chamber, empty at the moment. I contemplated the king's reaction if he knew Adrya spied on him carrying out the realm's private business.

Soft wind slid down the back of my shirt, making me straighten from the spy hole. I looked farther along the passage, but wind slapped my hair into my eyes, and I turned the other way. I motioned to Timur, who was leaning into the light from the spy hole, inhaling deeply. He closed his eyes and stayed where he was. "Come on," I urged. "You want to find a way out, don't you?" With a moan, he straightened and set off in the direction I pointed.

My own eagerness to get out was growing, given that neither Timur nor I knew where Rosin was at that moment.

We hadn't gone far before the passage slanted downward, the air grew chillier, and the stone wall felt increasingly damp. It was crumbling in places too, so loose stones skittered away when I dragged my foot over them. I felt my way carefully while Timur surged ahead. My hand slid over something slimy. I choked off my imagining of what it might be and wiped my fingers on my trousers, accidentally bumping the lump in my pocket. "Wait, Timur."

Timur's steps halted while I fished out the candle I'd taken from my room and the box of sulfur sticks from the Great Hall. I scraped the sulfur stick on the wall and lit the candle. After the deep dark, the small flame stung my eyes, but rough stone walls glimmered into sight. Timur squeaked like a rat and came back to snatch the candle from my hand. I tucked the sulfur sticks back in my pocket.

"Which way?" Timur asked.

"I don't know," I admitted.

Timur drew a steadying breath and led the way with me at his heels.

"The hallway turns." Timur swung left into a new passage.

As the candle he carried swept across what he judged to be a dead end, I saw the runes. "Wait. That's a door."

"Open."

I raised my hand, then hesitated, picturing us popping into sight in the Great Hall or Thien's bedchamber.

"Open!" Timur sounded as if he were choking.

I ran my hand down the runes and spoke the words. The door opened away from us, but not into a castle room or courtyard. Rather into a greyer darkness, softened by a faint glow near the floor. The sound of falling water rushed out to meet us. Timur grunted and pushed inside. The door began to swing shut behind him, and I scrambled through. Holding the candle over his head, Timur turned a full circle, scanning our surroundings. I inched forward, eyes on the odd glow. Timur came to stand next to me, and we both gazed down into the room's center. About ten feet below us, glittering water bubbled up into a rock pool, then flowed through twisting runnels to a middle and then a lowest pool, where it evidently drained away again.

I glanced up, seeking a gap through which light might be trickling to be reflected in the water, but darkness stretched away unbroken. With the hair stirring on the back of my neck, I lowered my gaze to the pool. It shimmered with what felt like the vibrations of elemental power; the same energy I'd felt when the courtyard fountain overflowed. I studied the pool. The rock formation looked natural, but it echoed the three-tiered shape of most of the fountains in Rin. Or rather, I suddenly realized, the other fountains echoed this ancient one—The Well of Sharing. It had to be. Unable to take my eyes off the water, I started down the narrow stairs winding along the curved wall. My crutch landed much too close to the edge. I pressed close to the wall.

Timur exclaimed and hurried after me. "Why are you going down there?"

I reached the bottom of the steps and hobbled toward

the fountain. The water rippled like music. I licked my lips. As certainly as if I'd read it in one of the old books in the library, I knew this well was the reason the Founders had built the castle here so it could be used by the Wys Ones, whose connection to the elements had been primitive and strong. From the ledge, the channels carrying the water from level to level had even looked like the old runes.

Timur scooped up a handful of the water and drank.

"No!" I cried.

Timur turned to me, chin dripping. "Why?"

I lifted a hand helplessly. "Just don't drink any more."

"Where are we?"

I eyed the circular room. "In the lowest level of the old tower, I think."

"Can we get out that way?" Timur stared upward.

"We could try going up, but there's only the one door out of the old tower, and it's through the jail, remember?"

"Then we have to go back." Timur took the stairs three at a time and bounced himself off the door. "How do I open it?"

I followed, touched the runes, and spoke. The door opened. As soon as Timur could squeeze through, he plunged into the passage, taking the candle with him. I glanced back at the well and slowly went after him. I'd come back here and look for signs of Rosin once I had Timur safely out and searching for Rosin elsewhere. Timur wasn't doing well. The candle was burning lower in his hand, and I smelled the sour reek of his fear sweat.

"Slow down," I said, "and put your hand on the wall again. If you want a door, we need to find runes."

"What's a rune?"

"Like the carvings on the door back there."

Timur put his free hand on the wall and slowed slightly. "The words open it?"

"Yes." I struggled to keep up. The passage ran endlessly, turning twice, but never yielding a spy hole or a door. Finally, Timur halted and waited for me.

"There's a stairway." Timur pointed. "Will we be trapped if we go up?"

"I don't think so."

Timur bounded up the stairs. I halted at the bottom, watching the candle fade to a dim glimmer. The stairwell loomed steep as a wall. The possibility of falling backwards held little charm. I swallowed my pride and crawled up on my knees, dragging my crutch. I emerged at the top, my own shirt damp under the armpits. The bubble of candlelight suggested passages stretching right and left.

Timur hovered at the corner.

I lifted a hand, filthy palm upwards. "Left?"

Timur went only a short way before he vanished around a corner, then popped back to whisper, "There's another one of those light holes here." He disappeared again as I hurried to catch up.

When I rounded the corner, Timur waited by the spear of light. I made out a lowered voice that I recognized as Rosin's and quivered with relief. I hadn't lost him completely after all. We must be in the same hallway I'd been in the day before, having entered from the opposite end.

"Door?" Timur murmured.

I shook my head. "Wait though." I put my eye to the hole. Rosin and Brylla sat knee to knee in chairs drawn up to face one another. Rosin's jerkin was unbuttoned and Brylla's hair was loose, as if they were both in the middle of changing for the mid-day dinner. They leaned close and spoke quietly.

"But if we take Lineth, will her presence protect us or stir Thien up?" Rosin said.

Brylla shrugged. "I'd say he wants to be rid of her. And while he doesn't want Beran to marry her, he won't want his son made unhappy by attacking us and risking her safety. Between that and her money, we'd be set."

"You really think so?" Rosin looked thoughtful.

She put her hand on his thigh. "I do. It's a perfect solution. And we'll have Dugan home again. I know he'll be happy to have Lineth in his bed, and you won't have to keep chasing some girl you don't care about." His mouth pinched as he looked down at her hand. "I'm still beautiful if you care to look, Rosin."

A soft thud sounded in the distant passageway, followed by the whisper of footsteps.

I pivoted toward Timur. "Adrya's coming," I whispered. "Hide. And put out the candle."

Timur gave me an unhappy look, but he blew out the candle and ghosted away from the spy hole. I hurried after him, hand on the wall, searching for a hiding place and finding only a jig in the stonework I pressed myself into it and waited, struggling to quiet my breathing.

I thought about what I'd just heard. Brylla was wrong—insanely so. If Rosin crossed the king, Thien would go after him like a wolf harrying sheep. He'd have to. After the betrayal by Lineth's father, Thien needed to show he was in control. He'd work all the vengeance on Rosin that I had ever hoped to see. I wouldn't have to convince the king to avenge the harm done to Rena, and other kids would be safe. But Rosin hadn't defied Thien yet, and if someone prevented him from taking Lineth, Thien would have no reason to punish him. So should I warn Adrya that he might go after Lineth? Or should I wait until Rosin acted? Assuming he did, of course. And what about Lineth? If I waited for Rosin to do something, would I endanger her? I gnawed my lower lip.

Farther down the passage where Timur had retreated, something scuffled over stone. I jerked to alertness, ready to jump out and swamp Adrya with an explanation of who Timur was and why he was there. The scuffling stopped. I tried to listen over the thunder of my heart. A soft brushing, then nothing. Had Timur just been scrambling to a better hiding place? What was going on?

I was ready to call his name when I heard steps again and realized that the opposite end of the corridor was growing lighter. I made myself as small as I could. The steps that approached were muted, but I recognized the brisk stride and was unsurprised when Adrya passed me and went right to the spy hole in Rosin's room. She peered through the hole, then drew back, shoulders sagging. I had time to notice that the murmur of voices in Rosin's room had ceased before Adrya turned to leave and looked straight at me.

She jerked as if she'd touched fire. Then she grabbed my arm and dragged me down the passage. "Hush," she said when I opened my mouth. By the moving light of Adrya's lantern, I scanned the passage as we hurried through it, but I saw no sign of Timur though we passed the place where he'd hidden.

"How did you get in here?" Adrya hissed.

"I tried using the runes until they worked," I said. Adrya's face screwed up in outrage. "Did you see anyone besides me?" I asked.

"No." Adrya's eyes widened. "You haven't told anyone else about the passages, have you? You promised me you wouldn't."

I hated confessing my failure to keep the passages secret, and I hated even more the idea of putting Timur's fate in Adrya's hands, but I couldn't leave Timur in the passages. Alone and in the dark, he'd be scared spitless.

"I didn't tell anyone exactly," I said, "but I took Timur into them."

"Who?" The lantern rattled in Adrya's hand.

"Another kid. He was in danger, so I had to hide him."

"What is wrong with you?" Adrya cried, then choked and asked more quietly, "What if he tells someone about them? What if he panics and makes enough noise that someone in one of the rooms hears him?"

"Then you're going to look a whole lot less insightful," I said. "We have to find him."

"Where did you last see him?" Adrya asked.

"Near where you found me."

"Why were you watching Rosin anyway? I told you I saw to it he didn't know enough to do what his uncle did."

I decided not to tell her what Rosin planned. Even if she believed me, she'd just stop him from snatching Lineth and send him home after Darklight.

Adrya moved back along the passage, turning from side to side, scanning all the shadowy spaces. We got all the way back to Rosin's room without seeing anything. She frowned at the passage beyond. "Did he go that way?"

"No, the way we just came."

We retraced our steps again, Adrya thrusting the lantern into every side passage as I softly called Timur's name, but we saw no sign of anyone.

Finally, Adrya stopped. "Could he have found a door and got out?"

"Maybe. He was there when I used the runes. But he's not quick with words, Adrya, and he's afraid of the dark."

Adrya spoke like a woman heavily put upon. "I'll have to go downstairs then. I'll be faster without you. I'll take you back to the library." She whirled and strode away.

I followed more slowly. I hoped Timur had escaped, but my stomach churned with worry. From some hidden source of air, a gust of wind ruffled the cobwebs overhead. I sniffed. Was that Adrya's perfume? I stiffened. It smelled like a mix of flowers and alcohol. It smelled like what I'd inhaled in my vision of Izzy searching for me at the castle.

# Chapter 17

ADRYA SHOVED ME through a narrow opening in the tunnel wall and then down a short corridor to a line of runes on the stones. She ran her hand along it, murmured the words, and escorted me into the library. Some distant sound echoed behind us. I twisted to see if Timur had followed but glimpsed no one.

"Did you smell anything in there?" I asked.

"Other than dust? No."

"Not something like…" I groped for words. "Sharp flowers?"

"Of course not. Don't leave this room," Adrya said grimly. "I need to speak to you. This time you've pushed too far." She opened the hidden door and vanished through it.

I lowered myself onto a stool, propped my crutch against the table, and rubbed my temples with both hands. "Pushed too far" sounded ominous. Panic rising in my chest, I lifted my gaze to scan the books and thought of them and my future as a Wysman being taken away. *Stop worrying about yourself*, I thought. *Timur's the one in trouble.* I pictured him breathing in light at a spy hole or trying to find the old tower again so he could huddle by that glowing well. What if he drank from it again? For all I knew, drinking would give him immortality, but I doubted it. Everything about that place screamed of twisted power. I grabbed my slate from the table and while I still remembered them, I drew the water channels from the well. They really did look like runes though not ones I knew. I studied them and waited.

The creak of the secret door made me look up as Adrya came back into the room alone.

"You didn't find him?" I let the slate drop.

Adrya shook her head. "He must have escaped. I looked everywhere." She dropped into her chair. "How could you have betrayed your promise to keep the passages secret?"

"I didn't mean to show him, and I don't think he'll tell anyone else. He doesn't know anyone else here. Adrya, Timur and I saw a well in what I think was the lowest level of the old keep. That's the Well of Sharing, isn't it?"

Adrya's eyes widened. "You were in there? That place is forbidden."

"Did you look for Timur in there?"

"I opened the door and glanced in, but he wasn't there. You shouldn't have gone in there, Jarka. My predecessor took me in once only, when he first showed me the passages. Then he forbade me to enter again, and unlike you, I listened to my teacher."

"It's where Rosin's uncle stole life from Ellyn's brother, isn't it?" I said.

"We're not talking about this anymore." She straightened and laid her palms flat on the table. "Enough is enough, Jarka. I was willing to overlook you taking your wind box back. I know what it means to you. But revealing the passages and spying on Rosin endangers Thien's rule. I can't have you as my apprentice any longer."

I'd been half expecting it, but still my heart stopped. "You can't mean that. Rosin didn't even know I was there."

"I *do* mean that. You don't have to leave the castle yet because Beran may have other uses for you, but you are no longer welcome to accompany me on my duties. In the meantime, I want to see this Timur and speak to him myself. Find him. He must understand how important it is that the passages be kept secret."

Acid swelled in my throat. I looked down and saw my slate chalked with what might be the last thing I ever learned from Adrya. I'd sacrificed my future for those chalk marks. I could only hope they meant something. "I'll go find Timur now, but first can you tell me what these runes mean?" I pushed the slate toward her.

Adrya slid her finger under the sketch of the channels leading from the top to the middle level of the well in the keep. "This one means 'from the giver.' It's complicated because you have to see the tail that means 'from' and the line here that turns 'give' into 'giver.' And the last one means 'flows the gift.' See the variation on 'give' again?"

I struggled for breath. "They really are runes?"

"Of course. Where did you find them?" Adrya bent over the slate, frowning. "As I recall, Dugan asked about these same runes just before I decided he wasn't suited to be my apprentice."

I stared at the top of her lowered head. Dugan had asked about the runes on the well and he'd done it months ago. That meant he had to know about the secret passages. Into my head popped the image of Dugan unexpectedly in our room when I first took Timur there. *Of course* Dugan knew, and he'd passed the knowledge to his father. Maybe Rosin had even charged him with ferreting out how to get in and out of them. After all, he claimed his uncle had blindfolded him. I thought it through. Dugan was in on this evil. His father would need help to manage a child and carry out the magic. Dugan had hidden the book where it would point to me, not him, and retrieved it when he needed it. Ice lodged in my gut as I thought of how sick Dugan looked. That was channeled power gone wrong and turning back on the one who tried to channel it. I realized Adrya was looking at me. "What?"

"Where did you find these runes?" she repeated.

"They're the marks on the well." I waited to see if she'd make the connection to Dugan.

Something flickered in her face until she looked away. "When you get hold of Timur, send him at once."

I pulled my crutch toward me and levered myself to my feet. With one last look around the library, I left.

*All right*, I thought. *That's done.* I should have known better than to let desire into my heart. I had to move on, the way I'd done when my mother died or when Clovyan beat me bloody. I shut all thought of being a Wysman out of my mind and considered what places in the castle Timur would both know and think safe. I'd send Timur to the library and then find and follow Rosin. As far as I was concerned, if Adrya was done with me, I was done with what I'd promised her.

Timur wasn't in the dorm, so I went out to the busy courtyard and swept my gaze over the crowd, especially near the tables by the kitchens. The young men who'd been in the yard's center earlier had moved to the edges and were watching a group of maidens milling near a pole with black and white ribbons fluttering from the top. The harassed looking steward was trying to sort out the ribbons and the maidens so dark and light would alternate. Thien's grinning minstrel waited to one side, lute in hand, ready to play the music to which the maidens would dance and weave the ribbons.

I didn't see Timur, but I did glimpse Lady Lineth coming through the castle gate, probably from the refuge, which meant her illness had passed. My worry for her increased.

The steward must have seen Lineth too because he called to her. "Come now, lady. We need another dancer."

The other would-be dancers saw Lineth and fell into wide-eyed silence. "That's the traitor's daughter, you fool," one said, then clapped her hand over her mouth when her words caromed around the stony yard.

The steward scowled. A different maiden pushed the rude girl aside. "Do join us, Lineth."

Everyone in the courtyard turned to look at Lineth. Her face flushed pink, but she stood even straighter than usual. "Thank you, but I believe I'll just watch." She slid to the edge of the crowd and walked toward the castle entrance. Ignoring the stares, I hobbled to meet her halfway. After a moment, people went back to watching the maidens.

"How are you, lady?" I asked quietly.

She pressed my arm. "Well enough now."

"Is Rena any better?"

"I'm afraid not."

I felt a moment of despair. Even if Thien punished Rosin, it wouldn't help Rena. It would be justice, I reminded myself. Justice mattered. It had to. I'd flung away everything I wanted by searching for it. "Have you by any chance seen Timur?"

Lineth looked at me sideways and smiled. "Ah, the mysterious Timur. No, I haven't."

From close behind us, a woman's voice said, "If you're talking about that horrible boy, I believe he fled the castle."

I turned to see Brylla, face pale, hands clenched tightly together. "Fled?" As far as I could see, Timur viewed the castle the way a rat might view a cheese shed. He'd never leave on his own.

"Yes. Who knows what he's done? He threatened my son." She thrust out her chin.

"I rather like Timur," Lineth said.

Brylla opened her mouth and then clamped it shut and drew a deep breath. "You're a generous woman, Lineth. Dugan was saying that just this morning. He admires you, you know."

Lineth tilted her head and raised one eyebrow. "He's gracious to have said so."

"You should come to our rooms this afternoon and drink tea," Brylla said.

"I...I thank you for the invitation of course, but I fear I'm busy today."

"Perhaps later." Brylla curtsied in Lineth's direction, gave me a look that slid away, and strolled out the gate, back stiff.

Lineth frowned after her. "What do you suppose that was about?"

"Don't go, lady," I said. "The Stonebridges have decided that marrying you to Dugan would solve all their problems. They've spoken to Thien about it." Since I was losing all my future as Adrya's apprentice, I no longer felt bound to keep her secrets.

"What? His Majesty didn't agree to that, did he?"

"No." I hesitated for only a moment. In for a lamb, in for a ram. "Thien plans to marry you off elsewhere." Under the sound of music and dancing, I told her about Lord Nithron's son. I let go of the idea of allowing the Stonebridges take Lineth so Thien would punish them. Lineth didn't deserve to be frightened and risked like that. "You need to stay away from the Stonebridges entirely. They're willing to take you by force if you won't go with them freely."

Her face went chalk white. I didn't blame her. "I must speak to His Majesty." She swayed, and I caught her elbow.

"You're going to the king?"

"Yes. It's time and past time."

I hesitated. I needed to find both Timur and Rosin, but Lineth's face was so pale I feared she might faint. "I'll escort you then."

She shot me a grateful look. We turned our backs on the dancers and went into the castle, leaving to the sound of horses clattering into the yard. *More nobles*, I thought. *Just what we need.*

"Are you going to tell the king something about Rosin?" If so, this delay wouldn't be in vain.

Lineth's fingers tightened, tugging my sleeve askew. "No, but Thien needs to know about something I've done, or rather, something Beran and I have done."

I closed my mouth down on the questions I wanted to ask. We halted long enough to learn from a door guard that the king was in the small audience chamber. A single guard stood outside the room.

"Will you tell the king I need to speak to him?" Lineth's voice was steady, but her fingers twitched on my arm.

The guard ducked inside, then reappeared. "He's busy, lady."

*Stone it.* Trying to think of where to leave Lineth, I started to draw her away, but she held firm. "Ask him again, please. It's important, or I wouldn't trouble him."

The guard grimaced but went back into the chamber. Then he came out and held the door open. I escorted Lineth in, and the guard closed the door. Thien was pacing the room. I scanned the wall, trying to judge where the spy hole must be but couldn't pick it out. Lineth leaned more heavily on my arm, her breath coming fast.

Thien regarded the two of us, frowning. Then his gaze settled on Lineth's pale face. "Are you unwell, lady?" He pointed to a chair against the wall, and I hastened to fetch it, but Lineth stayed on her feet.

"I beg your forgiveness, Your Majesty, but I have something I must tell you. I fear His Highness and I have put you in a difficult position."

Thien's face hardened. My knees went watery, but Lineth's backbone stayed arrow straight.

"How so?" Thien asked.

"Prince Beran and I have been handfasted since just before he left for the Westreach," Lineth said. "His bodyguard and your head orchard keeper stood as witnesses."

Handfasted? As in privately married? I felt an instant's horror. Then I had to stop myself from cheering.

For a few heartbeats, Thien didn't move. Then he took Lineth's elbow and helped her into the chair. He glanced over her shoulder at me. "Go. And hold your tongue."

Shamefully grateful for the excuse, I hustled out of the room. Sweet Powers, Lineth had guts. But Lineth as the wife of Rinland's prince was a wonderful notion. She'd be good for Beran and good for the country. Look at her willingness to help street kids in Rin. Of course, I recalled, she was not yet twenty and Thien was her guardian. If he wanted to annul Beran and Lineth's marriage, he could.

I put the thought out of my mind along with losing my place as Adrya's apprentice. I had a terrible fear that I'd find Timur and Rosin at the same time. Rosin had been plotting in his room when Timur first vanished, so he couldn't have taken him. But Dugan had been after us and could have followed us into the passage. What if Dugan had come across Timur and grabbed him? Timur was a year or two younger than I was. Maybe in Rosin's eyes, he still counted as someone worth stealing youth from. I had a sudden vision of the dead boy I'd seen when I went looking for Rena and Laren. Oh sweet Powers. The wind had warned me and I'd been too slow to understand. My heart thudding in my throat, I set off for the Stonebridges' rooms.

# Chapter 18

I KNOCKED, WAITED, then pounded. The door jerked open, and Dugan stood there, hand braced against the jamb. His eyes narrowed. "What do you want?"

For a moment, I was too shocked to speak. Dugan had looked ill in the courtyard a couple of hours ago, but now he looked as if the wall was the only thing holding him up. Dark half moons smudged the skin under his eyes. His cheeks looked sunken; his skin stretched thin over the bones.

"I'm looking for Timur," I finally said.

Dugan's elbow gave way, but he caught himself. "You think I'd let him in here? I'd be afraid of lice." Before I could answer, Dugan went on. "You're not fooling anyone, you know. He reeks of the streets, just like you. If he vanished and never came back, no one would miss him for an instant. Again like you." He gave a short laugh.

Every muscle in my body tightened with the urge to

knock Dugan flat. It wouldn't take much. Instead, I darted a look in either direction and leaned into the doorway so my face was a hand's breadth from Dugan's. He drew back.

"Did you do something to him in the passages?" I asked.

Dugan licked his lips. "What passages?"

"The ones that run all over the castle." I struggled to keep my voice down. "The ones that go from the dormitory to the well in the old keep to the spy hole into the room you're standing in."

Dugan's hand slipped again, and he collapsed to sit on the floor. "You think you know everything, you with your wind box." His voice was high, on the edge of hysteria.

I put out a hand to help him, but Dugan waved me off.

"People laugh at you behind your back," Dugan said. "Did you know that? You think Ellyn likes you? On the night of the dance, she agreed when I said your family kicked you out because you deserved it."

I froze, inside and out. "That's not true."

Even on the floor, Dugan managed a shaky smile. "It is true. Now go away, and leave me alone." He grabbed the edge of the door and slammed it shut.

I stared at the oak door as if it might open and Dugan might take back what he'd said, unsay it maybe, and make time run backwards, the way it sometimes did in the wind box.

"What are you doing here? The king told you to stay

away."

I swung around to see Brylla looking at me wide-eyed, holding her skirts away, as if they might be dirtied by brushing against my legs. "Where's your husband?" I demanded.

"He's gone out."

"To the refuge?"

"I don't know. Is Lineth there?" She laughed bitterly. "Now go away. Dugan and I have things to do." Her tone was oddly triumphant, as if she'd vanquished me.

"Gladly." I dodged around her, hobbled along the corridors, down the stairs, and across the courtyard. I had a vague sense of folks skipping out of my way.

One of the gate guards called to me as I passed. "Did you get the message the girl wanted you?"

I ignored him. I saw no one clearly until I saw Ellyn and Tally sitting on the front step of the refuge. Boys and girls swarmed between her and me, chased by a laughing girl I'd once pried from the hands of a woman to whom her mother had sold her. Several of the kids cried a greeting, but I walked between them to stand in front of Ellyn, who sprang to her feet when she saw me.

"Has Rosin been here?" I asked.

"No. You can't think I'd let him in. Wait." She turned to the other girl. "We're just going inside, Tally. I don't believe this is something the kids should hear." Tally nodded, and Ellyn hastened into the refuge.

I hobbled after her, my heart pounding.

She led me first to her room where Rena lay without moving, looking like a doll whose stuffing had come out. Even her braids drooped across the pillow. Laren was curled on the other bed, asleep. Ellyn tucked the blanket more tightly around him, then motioned me back into the main room.

"Have you found any proof Rosin did this?" she asked in a low voice.

Anger threatened to choke me. Timur was missing. I'd lost sight of Rosin. I'd lost everything. "No, but at least I'm trying."

She frowned. "Maybe you should tell the king what you think."

"Maybe you should have kept a better eye on Rena instead of dangling after Dugan," I heard myself say. "Even if you do agree with him that my family was right to kick me out."

She slapped me, catching me on the bruise Clovyan had left. I grabbed her wrist. We glared at one another.

A wail rose from her room, and I looked through the doorway to see Laren sitting up, watching us, his face crumpled in tears. Ellyn yanked free of my grip and hurried over to gather him up and carry him out into the main room. Over Laren's head, her eyes met mine, burning with fury. I turned a little away.

Between two beds, a line of dark spots ran down the castle wall against which the refuge was built. My breath caught. I moved toward them, hand out. How could I have been so stupid? Not spots. The worn remnants of runes. I stopped, hand hovering an inch from the wall.

Laren's sobs dwindled to hiccups.

"What are you doing?" Ellyn asked.

Adrya would choke on her wine if I told more people about the passages, but a door was right here, and Rosin was loose to do as he liked. It was amazing how free I felt with all hopes gone.

"Watch." I drew my hand down the runes, reciting the words. The door opened, then drifted shut again.

"No! No!" Laren shrieked. "That's where the Grabber lives."

"Is this where you and Rena saw him?" I asked.

Laren nodded and stifled a sob. Snot left a slimy trail on his upper lip.

"Sweet Powers," Ellyn whispered. "That's how someone snatched Rena."

"I think that someone was Rosin but I'm afraid it could have been Dugan. Rena said whoever she saw was big, and that fits both of them. I think he's helping his father. I'm going to tell the Tower Guards and see if they'll post someone here. You're not safe without some protection." I started toward the door to the street.

"Jarka."

I turned back.

Ellyn stroked Laren's head. "Your family treated you badly. Dugan is lying if he says I said otherwise."

Something loosened in my chest. "I'm sorry for what I

said. You look after these kids like a mother bear."

She smiled faintly, then buried her face in Laren's hair.

I hastened out the door, along the street, and around the corner, then slammed to a halt. Clovyan leaned toward one of the gate guards, who had lowered his pike and was speaking in a flat voice. "Stop shouting. We've sent for him. Move to one side and wait."

"I don't have time to waste waiting," Clovyan said.

I forced myself to move forward. "You looking for me, Clovyan?"

Clovyan rounded on me. "Where's Izabeth?"

I'd thought I was already as scared as I could get. I'd been wrong. "What do you mean? Isn't she home?"

"No. She ran off while I was out having my morning ale. Only bit of comfort I get, and the brat takes advantage. Lyssa says she probably went looking for you, and one of the neighbors saw her heading this way."

"You're talking about the little girl who was looking for him?" The gate guard nodded toward me.

"Where is she?" Clovyan demanded.

The guard jerked his thumb along the wall toward the corner by the refuge. "She squatted over there for hours, then vanished a little while ago. We thought she'd gone home. We sent for Jarka after prayers, but he didn't come."

My breath stopped. It had been Izzy, not Lyssa, who'd come to the castle that morning. I'd ignored her message and now she'd vanished.

"She must be keeping out of sight, playing when she's supposed to be pulling basting threads," Clovyan said. "When I get hold of her, I'll teach her not to dodge work."

I grabbed Clovyan's arm. "Breathe hard in her direction, and I'll make you sorry."

Clovyan swung his fist. I dodged, but his knuckles still grazed the side of my head. Before I had time to plan it, I lowered my shoulder and plowed into his chest sending him stumbling back.

"Here!" The guard pushed between us. "You're disturbing the king's peace."

From the corner of my eye, I glimpsed the second gate guard stepping back a pace or two and looking into the yard. He shoved his fingers between his teeth and whistled.

"This is all your fault, Jarka," Clovyan shouted over the guard's shoulder. "I mean to tell Lyssa it's you she should blame, not me." His eyes narrowed. "She'll never forgive you."

"Probably not. And that will make two of us."

"Go home." The guard shoved the shaft of his pike into Clovyan's stomach. "We'll search the castle for your daughter and bring her home."

"She's not his daughter," I said. "Clovyan, if you hurt Izzy or Lyssa, I swear I'll ensorcell you so your nightmare-begotten privates fall off."

Braced against the shaft of the guard's pike, Clovyan went ashen. Cold resolve solidified in my chest. Why hadn't I thought of that before? Behind Clovyan's scorn for my wind reading, he must always have been afraid. Clovyan pushed on the pike, trying to shove it aside. At that moment, half a dozen guards poured out the gate. I saw Clovyan shoved face down on the stones with a guard on his back a heartbeat before a guard flung me down too. My crutch clattered away. My bruised cheek scraped on a cobble.

"Get off me!" Clovyan shouted. "This is all his fault." I knew enough to stay down, but not Clovyan. He bucked and tried to unseat the man.

The gate guard glanced over his shoulder at me. "Let him up. The other one's the troublemaker."

It was as if my fantasy of siccing the Tower Guards on Clovyan had come true right when I'd given up on making it happen. A guard removed himself from my back. I reached for my crutch and struggled to my knees and then my feet. Two guards grabbed Clovyan's arms and hauled him up, still shouting. "Stone you and everyone in this castle!"

"Shut it," one of the guards said. The reinforcements dragged him through the gate, leaving only the one who'd been arguing with Clovyan to start with.

Staring after Lyssa's husband, I drew a shaky breath. She'd be frantic over Izzy missing, of course, but when she had time, she'd be furious at me for getting Clovyan arrested. I'd never live in her house again. Another piece of my past—and future—gone, I thought with a sinking despair.

I turned to find the gate guard focusing on me. His narrowed eyes did not suggest respect for my innocence. I backed up a step.

"You'd threaten sorcery like that right in front of me when someone bewitched a kid only two nights ago? I'm sending for the captain."

"There's no such thing as 'sorcery,' I was just threatening him. Go ahead and send for the captain. You can tell him how a girl disappeared right under your nose."

The guard's eyebrows drew together.

"When she was here waiting, were there other folks around?" I asked.

"Plenty of them. Visitors who are staying in town have been coming in and out all day."

I rubbed my hand down my face. When had that sweat coated my skin? "You're needed in the refuge. There's a hidden door into it from the castle. I think that's how someone got hold of the little girl I found in the old keep."

"I can't leave my post, and if I could, I wouldn't do it at your bidding."

"Then send for more reinforcements. That door makes what happened in the refuge into castle business."

The lines between the guard's brows faded. He darted into the shadow under the gate and called for a page, then stepped aside to let a group of well-dressed men come from the castle toward where I waited. Among them, dressed in black and white silk, walked Rosin.

I shouldered a man aside and rocked to a halt, blocking Rosin's path. Rosin blinked and drew back.

"Where is she?" I asked.

"Who?"

"Izzy! The little girl you grabbed from over there!" I jabbed a finger toward where Izzy had crouched.

Rosin's face went milk-white.

The man I'd pushed crowded close. "Do you need help, Rosin?"

Rosin grabbed my elbow. "Go on. I'll catch up." The other men drifted down Kings Way, glancing back at us, and muttering to one another. Rosin waited until they were out of earshot, then leaned close and spoke low, his breath scented with the anise he'd chewed to sweeten it. "My uncle was the one who did the channeling. It was years ago, and he paid when he died. I admit I was the one who gained, but I was blindfolded. I didn't even know what he was planning."

I stared into Rosin's contorted face. "You're talking about years ago."

"I just said that!"

"I don't care about what happened then. What have you done with Izzy?"

"I've done nothing," Rosin whispered fiercely. "Look at me! Do I have fewer wrinkles, less gray hair? I've not stolen a day from a dog."

The guard came closer, probably expecting another fight. This time involving a lord he might be forced to arrest.

Rosin's voice rose, high and hysterical. "I'm not staying here any longer. This is getting out of hand." He whirled and all but ran back into the castle.

The guard looked immensely relieved. As I turned to face him, my eye caught on something white fluttering in the crack between a cobblestone and the bottom of the wall. I balanced on my good leg and bent cautiously to hook my finger around a silk kerchief. When I straightened, I caught a scent and raised it to my nose. Flowers, and something sharp. My head swam, and I jerked the kerchief away. It was the same smell I'd inhaled in the passages when Timur went missing. The smell I'd sensed in my vision of Izzy coming to the castle.

Once, when Lyssa's first husband, a sailor, had been alive, he'd come back from a trip to Lac's Holding and told a story about ships from elsewhere seizing men on the docks and forcing them to work as seamen. I'd been fascinated and nagged for details. How had grown men been taken so easily? The kidnappers had knocked them out, I learned, using rags soaked in some drug that smelled of something flowery. Lyssa's husband had joked that was why he didn't buy flowers for Lyssa.

"What's that?" the guard asked.

I closed my fist over the kerchief. "This is how Izzy could be seized right out in the open. With people coming and going, all Rosin had to do was clap this over her face and carry her off like a kid who'd been dragged out of bed too early."

I went back to the refuge, where Tally had the kids lined up outside holding hands, two by two.

"You're leaving?" I asked.

"We're going to New Square for the puppet show there." She sounded so unconcerned that I figured Ellyn hadn't told her about the secret door, but instead had acted to get the kids out of harm's way.

I hurried into the refuge. Ellyn was in the rocking chair crooning to Laren who slumped against her, fast asleep.

"A guard will be here soon," I said.

Her breath eased out. "Thank you. I sent the others away for now."

I offered her the kerchief. "Don't inhale too much, but think. Could you have smelled something like this when your little brother was taken?"

She leaned over Laren and took a cautious sniff. Then she recoiled, eyes wide. "I don't know. It was a long time ago. But maybe."

"I think that's how you were knocked off guard. Not sorcery. I don't think you can 'ensorcell' someone, though I just threatened to do it to my cousin's husband. Why Rosin's uncle took your brother instead of you, I don't know. Maybe he wanted a boy or just someone as young as possible."

"Sweet Powers," Ellyn murmured.

I tucked the kerchief into my pocket and limped down the room to take a lantern from the chimneypiece and light it with a spill from the fire.

"What are you doing?" she asked.

"My cousin Izzy is missing. She and Rena were both at the castle, in Rosin's reach, because of me, and they're both in danger because I was too stupid to see what was right in front of me, even with the wind's warning. Timur too." I put my hand on the top rune. "They can't wait for whatever the king might or might not do."

At that moment, a guard strode through the doorway, looming like a giant over the row of small beds. "What's this nonsense about some secret way in here from the castle?"

"Watch." I ran my hand down the runes and spoke the words.

The guard's jaw dropped. "Stone me," he breathed.

"Your job is to stop anyone from coming through this door." I took a single step before Ellyn rose from rocker saying, "Wait, Jarka." She carried the sleeping Laren to the small room and returned. "I'm going with you."

"It's too dangerous. Think of what happened to Rena."

"Think of what happened to my brother." She shoved her face close to mine. "I let that happen once, and I'm never doing that again."

I wanted to push her away, keep her safe, but I couldn't do that to her. The fierce need in her face and voice was too familiar. I nodded.

The door had swung shut by now, so I opened it again. I looked over my shoulder at the guard. "There are two little kids in the back room. Keep an eye out," I said. He looked as alarmed at the thought of minding kids as he had when the door opened. I followed Ellyn into the passage and the door shut behind us.

With me holding the lantern high, Ellyn and I entered every side passage we came to and searched for what Adrya had to have missed. I tried to map our progress in my head, but it was too confusing. We turned into yet another hallway and surged forward until the lantern showed that it ended at a crossing passage. "There!" Ellyn cried and darted left where a patch of deeper darkness, blotched with something pale, stretched across the floor. I hurried after her and thrust out the lantern.

It was Timur, flat on his back, unmoving.

I thudded to my knees and bent over him. "Timur? Timur, it's me." The lantern light gleamed off slits of eyes beneath lids not quite closed. My heart clenched. I put a hand on Timur's chest, then yanked it away. He throbbed with the same wrong power Rena had. I forced myself to put my hand back. For a long moment I waited, but his chest never lifted. His breath never brushed over my fingers. Someone gave a strangled cry, and I realized it was me.

Ellyn shouldered me aside and pressed her ear to Timur's chest. Her face was turned toward me, and I saw the truth spread over it.

"Sweet Powers. Sweet Powers," I mumbled, maybe a prayer, maybe a protest. "Oh, Sweet Powers." I had a sudden memory of telling Timur that he wouldn't need a knife in the castle. I rocked on my knees and stared into the darkness.

# Chapter 19

"I'M SO SORRY, Jarka." Ellyn slid her arm around my shoulder. "He's a friend?"

"I brought him here."

"You couldn't have known."

"I told him I needed him to watch my back. I saw death in my wind box! Of course I knew." I sagged back on my heels. "But I wanted him here. I wanted someone on my side." I felt overwhelmingly tired.

"What killed him?" Ellyn murmured. "Was it the same as my brother? He's not...dried up." Her soft voice quivered.

I drew a breath and when I did I caught a whiff of the same drug that was on the kerchief in my pocket. Of course he smelled of that, I thought. How else could Dugan have grabbed him? Timur would have fought like the street rat he was.

"By the feel of him, he's been where there's crooked

power, but I don't think it killed him. For all I know, he feels of it because he drank it."

"What?"

"He drank from the Well of Sharing, which is where I need to go." Fueled by a surge of fury, I shoved to my feet.

"Can you find it?" Ellyn asked.

"I have to. It might not be too late for Izzy." I touched Timur's hand. "I have to take the lantern, but you should stay here." My throat swelled. "Keep Timur company in the dark."

"I'm coming with you," she said steadily. She put her hand over mine on my crutch. "It's taken me a long time to learn this, but it's the living we owe, not the dead. Besides if your cousin can't walk, you'll need help carrying her."

I closed my eyes and drew a deep breath because with her words I knew I needed company in the dark too. Maybe we all did. I gestured with the lantern, and we had just started down the crossing passage when somewhere behind me, a muffled voice spoke and I recognized Rosin.

"I think this is the way. I haven't been in here in years, and even then I was blindfolded during the last part."

It was Lineth who answered. "You don't have to do this, you know. We can still go back. I wouldn't tell Thien."

Feeling strangled, I swung around and saw lantern glow emerging from a side passage. I nudged Ellyn back to where Timur lay, shuttered my lantern, and set it down so

I'd at least have one hand free.

"It will all work out, my dear. Don't worry. I've been planning to divorce Brylla for some time, and I'll be a good husband to you."

It took me three heart beats to take in that Rosin intended to marry Lineth himself, not unite her with Dugan. With that knowledge came a flare of savage glee. If Timur and Rena and, the Powers damn me, Izzy never spoke again, I had no way to prove Rosin had harmed them, but in snatching Lineth, Rosin was doing something he couldn't deny. Thien would come down on him like a rock slide.

I edged toward the corner and peered around it in time to see Rosin enter the passage, one arm holding up a lantern and the other wrapped around Lineth. In the lantern light, her hands gleamed where they gripped Rosin's sleeve. Her eyes were wide, her face a sick white. Ellyn's fingers spasmed in the back of my shirt. I pulled free and stepped out in front of Rosin and Lineth. "Let her go."

Rosin jumped back. He wore a sword, but when the arm wrapped around Lineth flicked, a knife pointed to her throat. "I would regret having to cut my future wife, but I will if you don't get out of the way." His voice shook. So did the knife.

From the corner of my eye, I saw Ellyn pull her own knife. I backed up, gripping Ellyn's arm and pulling her with me. A knife fight between her and Rosin was the last thing we needed. For one thing, explaining to Thien how one of his lords came to be stabbed would be unpleasant. "Lineth is right, you know. If you let her go, you'll be clean of all blame."

"Get out of the way," Rosin said.

Keeping hold of Ellyn, I leaned against the wall and raised the point of my crutch to fend him off. "Where's Izzy?"

"I told you I have no idea who you're talking about," Rosin said. "But I've had enough. I'm leaving."

"Not with Lady Lineth." Waving her knife, Ellyn tore herself free of my grip and pushed past me. "The gate guards will see she doesn't want to go."

He smiled patronizingly. "The gate guards won't see a thing. As you've perhaps noticed, we aren't near the gates. My uncle knew a way out through these passages."

The last time I'd seen Lineth, she'd been swaying on her feet in Thien's small audience chamber. Now, she looked as if her grip on Rosin's arm was the only thing holding her up. "I know the way too," I said. "Release Lineth, and I'll tell you which way to go."

"Tell me, and I won't cut her."

I was almost sure he was bluffing. Nothing I'd seen of Rosin suggested he had the guts to go after someone anywhere near his own size. I thought of Timur and knew 'almost sure' wasn't good enough. Lineth needed to get away from him. "You're nearly there." I pointed down the passage. "Straight down there. The door's just a regular door. You won't have any trouble getting out. Now let Lineth go, or I'll make you."

Dragging Lineth with him, Rosin backed into the passage, eyes still on me and Ellyn. "If you come after me, I'll hurt her."

Lineth squirmed in his grip, and I could feel Ellyn quivering. I held my breath.

Rosin backed up another step and caught his heel against Timur's ribs. With a smothered cry, he toppled backward. His lantern flew up, leaving a streak of light in the blackness. Lineth tore herself out of his loosened grip and stumbled to brace one hand against the wall and bend over and vomit.

Rosin scrambled to his feet, knife in hand.

"Go," I told him. "Run. Leave us alone, and we won't tell Thien."

"Like Nightmare we won't." Ellyn scooped up a loose stone and flung it at him. She dived for another. He raised his hand to shield himself.

"Ellyn, please!" *The Powers save me from fierce Rinnish women.* "Lord Rosin, if you hurry, it will be too late for us to tell because you'll be gone."

Ellyn shrieked and flung a rock the size of a baby's fist.

Rosin snatched up his lantern and ran.

Ellyn charged after him. I grabbed her wrist. "Stop!"

"You let him get away!" she cried. "You told him how to escape!"

"I lied. I don't know how to get out of the castle from

down here. In the meantime, he's left my cousin somewhere and we have to find her. Can you get the lantern?"

Ellyn halted, chest heaving with fury. She snatched up the lantern and opened it.

"Lineth," I asked over my shoulder, "are you ill?"

"Not really," she said faintly.

"Can you find your way out on your own?" I asked.

Still bent over, she shook her head.

"Then can you wait here while we look for my cousin?" I asked.

"I'll come with you," she said.

I didn't want to take Lineth into more danger. "Timur is here," I said. "He's dead."

Still trembling, Lineth straightened and stared at Timur's body.

"Someone needs to stand vigil over his body. Until the next dawn, he shouldn't be alone. You know that."

"Lineth," Ellyn said gently, "you don't have the right to take risks." For a long moment, she held Lineth's gaze.

So Ellyn suspected the same thing I did. I feared for Lineth but couldn't help feeling glad, too. If Lineth was pregnant, that would make it much harder for Thien to annul her marriage to Beran. No kingdom needed a chance child of the future king running around.

Lineth drew a deep breath, but her voice still shook. "Very well. We can't stay here though, not if Rosin might come back. Where can I hide with him?"

"Try to find a stairway and drag him in there. Don't go too far though. It's easy to lose your way."

She nodded.

I reminded myself that Izzy's fate was in my hands and forced the next words out. "We have to keep searching, so I can't leave the lantern. It will be dark."

"Then Rosin won't see us." Lineth crouched next to Timur. "Go."

I took the lantern and swung it into the crossing passage. As I did, a breeze fluttered past me, pushing me that way. Thank the Powers. The breeze led me and Ellyn as if it were a map. I felt unutterably grateful to Ellyn for threading this maze with me. We followed the wind as the passage dipped. Ahead the darkness paled. The well, I realized, and the door must be ajar, caught on a loose stone maybe. What's more, the room looked as if it was lit by more than the shimmer of the fountain.

From beyond the doorway, a shrill voice pierced the gloom. "I tell you I have the chant right this time."

"That wasn't Dugan, was it?" Ellyn whispered.

"I think it was." We crept forward.

"You said you had it right before," a woman said, "and you turned out to be wrong. Not surprisingly, I suppose. You couldn't even snatch a messenger boy who was half your size out of the street with no one around. If I hadn't heard the page say this little slut was outside the gate, we'd have no-one." Brylla. Of course it was Brylla. Talking about the dead boy I'd seen in the wind box at the start of all this. My understanding of events spun like the Darklight wheel and came up with a different figure at the top. Not Rosin. Brylla. Brylla, whose husband scorned her because she lacked the youth he'd stolen, who failed to love her and would send her away.

And she was talking about Izzy. My heart threatened to block my throat and choke me.

I shuttered my lantern and set it down. Ellyn pulled the door toward us until the gap was wide enough to squeeze through. On the lip of the opening, my crutch slid, and pebbles skittered away like mice. I froze, but Dugan and his mother went on, absorbed in their own quarrel.

"We might not get another chance," Brylla said. "Your stoning father ran through my money. If he leaves me now, I'll be destitute, sent home to tend my aging parents. I am *not* letting that happen."

"I tell you it will work this time," Dugan said. "You think I'd take a chance? You've seen what the channeling does to me when I get it wrong."

As I inched forward, the sunken space in the tower's center slowly revealed itself, lit by three lanterns, the flickering points of a triangle. On one side of the well stood Dugan, looking even more ghastly in the lantern light coming from below. On the other was Brylla, clad only in a white shift.

My gaze narrowed from the room's edges to its center and the limp figure lying in the middle pool. Izzy's head was propped on the pool's stone lip, but the water washed over her body, darkening her russet gown to the color of old blood, the skirt trailing in the stream that flowed to the lowest pool. Her hands and feet were tied, her eyes closed. She lay as still as Timur.

My legs turned to stone. When Izzy twitched and whimpered, I nearly fell to my knees.

"Make her breathe more of the sleep spirits," Brylla said.

Dugan moved closer to Izzy, pulling a kerchief from his pocket. He lifted one of her eyelids, and I bit back a protest at his touching her. "She's still under. You want her alive, don't you? Too much and she'll end up like that Timur." He tucked the kerchief loosely into his belt.

"I *need* her alive," Brylla said. "What good would she be to me otherwise?" She crossed her arms and rubbed her bare shoulders. "It's chilly in here. Get on with it."

"We stop this now," I whispered.

Ellyn snatched up a rock and flung it to bounce off the side of Dugan's head. He howled and bent over, one hand clapped to the spot where the stone had hit him. Before he stopped wailing, I was half down the stairs, cursing my slowness. Ellyn flashed past me, knife in hand. She jumped the last two steps and lunged straight at Brylla. Brylla had time only to widen her eyes and lift her hands before Dugan grabbed Ellyn from behind, pulled the kerchief from his belt, and clapped it over her face.

"Let her go!" I cried, having finally reached the bottom of the stairs. I hurled myself toward him, but he swung around so Ellyn was between us. Right in front of me, I saw her eyes roll back, saw her sag in his grip. Brylla lunged to pick up the knife that clattered from Ellyn's fist. I smothered a moan. Slowly Dugan lowered the kerchief. Ellyn's full weight was draped over his arm, and big as he was, he was weak enough to stagger and lean against the wall.

For a long, silent moment, Brylla, Dugan, and I stood staring at one another. Brylla strolled toward me. I glared into her face, marked with a knowing smile. I hated her.

"Guards are on their way here," I said. "If you leave now, you might get away."

"Oh, I don't think so," Brylla said. "If guards are coming, why would you be here with just the girl? In truth, I think the Powers sent you to channel water for me."

I couldn't believe the Powers didn't instantly send fire, flood, and storm to punish her blasphemy. "Not likely!"

"Very likely," Brylla said cheerfully, "because if you don't, Dugan will kill her." She handed the knife to Dugan.

Barely able to breathe, I twisted to look at Izzy. Her lips were blue. I had to get her and Ellyn both out of there. "What do you want me to do?"

"Dugan recited a chant he learned from an old book. Something about power and letting it go. I don't remember exactly."

"I know the one," I bluffed, "and I know how to do this. I even know what Dugan was probably doing wrong." I met Brylla's skeptical gaze. What would make her believe me? "Four tower coins, lady, and your promise that I go free after I've done it."

Her face relaxed into a smile. Just what she expected from street trash. "Of course."

*Liar.*

"What must we do?" Brylla asked.

"Untie Izzy," I said.

"Who?"

I choked back my fury and jerked my head toward the fountain. "Her. The giver has to be free, or it's not a gift." That was probably a lie, but I kept my voice as cool as I could. If they thought I cared about Izzy, they'd smell a rat.

"Do it yourself," Brylla said.

I propped my crutch on the edge of the fountain and struggled with the wet knot around Izzy's ankles. At least some heat of life still warmed her legs. When the rope yielded, I moved to where I could reach her wrists, all the while trying frantically to think of how to get Ellyn and Izzy out of there unharmed any more than they already were.

"Now you lie in the bottom pool, lady," I said.

Brylla clambered over the edge of the lowest pool. She sat in the water and gave a small shriek. "It's so cold."

I could see that in the goose flesh on her arms. The cold didn't stop her from lying down though. Her white shift turned almost transparent as the water flowed over her. I thought I might never want to kiss a girl again.

I glanced at Ellyn. Dugan had slid down the wall to sit on the floor. Ellyn was propped beside him, much too close to the tip of her own knife in his hand.

"Now don't move, or this won't work." I turned my attention to Izzy. The water bubbled into the top pool, then ran over through the carved runes and over her to Brylla. I gripped the fountain with both hands. "Don't let Dugan interrupt either," I told Brylla. "You've seen what flawed channeling can do, and you don't want anything bad to happen to you, right?"

"You heard him, Dugan," Brylla said sharply. "Keep away."

Dugan made a sound like a strangled sob.

I began reciting the chant I'd seen in the book hidden under my bed. I'd only glimpsed it, so I wasn't sure. If I got it wrong, I didn't know what would happen, but I didn't know what else to do. "My heart leaps with power." I hauled myself up and over the fountain's edge until I knelt in the basin with Izzy. The water was cold enough to make me flinch, and the stone was hard and uneven under my knees, but I crept forward. "I open my hand and let my power go." I slipped my arms under Izzy and cradled her to my chest. Brylla watched me intently.

Izzy was out of the water now, which I could only hope meant she was safe. I kept on chanting. If I got it right, I would give Brylla what she wanted from my own body, and then she'd have no need of Izzy.

"It's working!" Brylla cried. "I feel it working."

Water rushed over me and onto her.

As if someone had tipped an oil lamp over into a fire, heat burned through me. My vision wavered. That far away, chanting voice wasn't mine, was it?

Brylla shrieked. "Fire! The wheat field is on fire!"

In a daze, I turned my head to look at her. She sat up, eyes wide with terror, looking at something only she could see. She gripped her temples. "A thief is in the shop. The baby is a girl. The ship is sinking," she moaned. She turned to look at Dugan. "Make it stop," she pleaded.

He struggled to his feet and rushed to her side. As he did, Ellyn leapt up and reeled to the edge of the fountain. She put out her arms for Izzy. "Hurry!" she cried. I tipped Izzy into her embrace, slid from the fountain, grabbed my crutch, and hauled myself up the stairs after Ellyn. At the door to the dark passageway, she waited.

"You monsters!" Dugan's voice was husky as if he were crying. "I'll kill you both!"

"Help me, Dugan!" Brylla cried.

"Go, Ellyn!" I said.

Instead, she nudged me into a side passage where I stumbled and crashed to the floor, sending a shock of pain through both knees. She crouched next to me, with Izzy in her arms.

The door to the well room opened wider, spilling light into the passage, outlining Dugan's bulk. From the room came Brylla's babbling voice. "She has a lover. The boy is still here. The old man is dying. Don't leave me, Dugan!"

With a curse, he turned back.

Ellyn and I wasted no time helping one another up and fleeing into the dark.

# Chapter 20

NEARLY WEEPING WITH relief, I slid through the hidden door into the old keep courtyard with Ellyn right behind me, carrying Izzy. Too late, I'd realized we forgot our lantern at the well, and in the dark passages, I'd somehow managed to get turned around. We'd seen nothing of Lineth.

"Thank the Powers." Ellyn sagged against the wall, blinking in the sudden sunlight. She'd shifted Izzy to her hip as soon as the kid started to come round, but her arms still had to be tired. Dirt smudged her forehead where she'd shoved away a stray curl. She was fierce and safe and utterly beautiful. Izzy buried her face in Ellyn's neck. Her soaked gown clung to her, and her hair hung in rat tails.

"It's all right, short stuff." I pinched her foot. "We'll get you home to your ma in no time." I suppressed a cringe at the idea of explaining to Lyssa what happened to both Clovyan and Izzy.

We headed toward the voices in the main courtyard. I'd get someone to fetch Lyssa. Then I'd leave Izzy with Ellyn and go to Adrya for help in retrieving Lineth and dealing with all three Stonebridges. In the gateway between the two yards, I scanned for someone to send to Lyssa. Maidens no longer danced with the Darklight ribbons, but the main courtyard still teemed with merrymakers. A group of guards, Gelas among them, milled about near the stables, waving ale mugs around and talking over one another in loud, quick words.

Gelas' gaze caught on me. "Hey!" he called. "What are you doing with her?" He started our way. "Is this like with the refuge girl?"

The other guards trailed after him, drifting along at first, then picking up speed until they were running. Ellyn clutched Izzy to her chest, and I moved between her and them. The men crowded near us, an arm's length away, panting hard, faces tense.

"It's sorcery." White showed all around the edges of Gelas' eyes. "He's the one I told you about. The gate guard said he threatened to work sorcery, and now he's spelled that little girl."

"Sorcerer," someone said, voice full of horror.

A guard snatched Izzy from Ellyn before I realized his intent. She screamed and thrashed in the man's arms. I took a step toward them, but hands slammed me back against the stone wall. Gelas leaned his forearm across my throat, pinning me.

"What did you do, sorcerer?" Gelas cried, sending a cloud of ale fumes up my nose. Dark spots danced in my vision.

"Leave him alone," Ellyn cried. "He didn't hurt her. He saved her."

Gelas narrowed his eyes at her. "You were there when the other girl was hurt too. Are you in on this?"

Another guard put his hand on Gelas' shoulder. "He's Adrya's apprentice, Gelas. Take care."

"He's a sorcerer." Gelas eased his arm off my throat but jabbed a finger in my direction. "He hurt that little girl."

"I didn't." I wheezed air into my chest.

Izzy was screaming in the guard's arms. "Jarka! Jarka!"

"Izzy!" cried a woman.

Izzy and I both turned toward the familiar voice, and Lyssa pushed past the guards with her arms out. Izzy hurled herself from the guard's arms to her mother's.

Lyssa swayed and murmured in Izzy's ear before turning an angry face toward me. "What have you done, Jarka?"

I raised my hands, palms out. "I didn't hurt her. You know I never would."

"Of course not," she said. "I'm talking about Clovyan. The guard says he's been arrested. Maybe that makes you happy, but how are we going to eat?"

I distantly heard Ellyn make a low sound of protest. "We." When Lyssa said "we," she didn't include me. Some last bit of childhood broke in my chest.

"I don't know," I said. "But Clovyan threatened to beat Izzy for running off. I can't let that happen. I'll help you, but first I have to talk to Adrya or maybe even the king. I have news about Lady Lineth. And Lady Brylla is hurt. The king will want to know."

She popped her mouth scornfully. "You'll never be done here. You'll always have one more thing to do."

Ellyn put a hand on Lyssa's arm. "I was there when Jarka found Izzy. Why don't you come to the refuge with me? We can get Izzy warm and dry while I tell you about it."

Without a backward look, Lyssa let herself be turned away from me and led toward the gate.

Ellyn took a moment to say, "You're doing the right thing."

My chest felt too tight to breathe, and Gelas was waiting for me.

"For once you're right," he said. "The king needs to hear what you've been up to." He took my arm and hustled me toward the castle entry, waving for two other guards to catch up. A door guard told us that Thien was in the small audience chamber, and Gelas dragged me through the doorway.

I barely noticed. Adrya had already told me I no longer had a place with her. I no longer had a place with Lyssa, and I knew now I hadn't had one for a long time. I'd finally admitted to myself that I left her house as much because I was angry with her as because of Clovyan's beating.

We turned the corner to the audience chamber where two guards stood outside the closed door. From inside came the muffled sound of Thien's raised voice, answered to my surprise, by Prince Beran's. "I wouldn't just leave her. I couldn't." The door opened, and Beran stood in the doorway, slapping riding gloves against his thigh and looking uncharacteristically grim. "His Majesty wishes to speak to Adrya," he told one of the guards. The man took off.

The prince's slanted brows drew down in a frown at me and Gelas. "What's this?"

"The boy's been practicing sorcery, sir," Gelas said. "Something unnatural has been going on. He's hurt kids in ways the healer doesn't understand."

"He'd never do that," Beran said.

"I didn't, but kids *have* been hurt. What's more, Lady Lineth—" I chose my words carefully. No need to blurt out news of the passages in front of the guards. "She needs help."

Beran took a step toward me. "What's happened?" Thien appeared in the doorway, and Beran turned to him. "Something's amiss with Lineth."

I pulled against Gelas' hold. "Please, Your Majesty. Lady Lineth's in danger, and I have something to tell you about the Stonebridges too."

For a dizzy moment, I met the king's sharp gaze.

"Come in, Jarka," Thien said at last. "The rest of you may go."

"Sir, this concerns Lineth," Beran said. "I wish to stay."

Thien's mouth tightened, but he said, "Of course."

Gelas gave one final squeeze and then released his hold on my arm. As he walked away, Adrya appeared. "A guard told me I was needed."

"You are." Thien went back into the room. I followed with Adrya and Beran. Gesturing Adrya and Beran into chairs, Thien sat. "Let's hear it. I have other matters to tend to."

I drew a deep breath. It was time to find out whether Thien would punish evil when he could no longer deny it. "The first thing you need to know is that the Stonebridges have learned to use the Well of Sharing and they've been trying to do it. Passages to it run behind the walls of the castle."

Adrya flinched. I didn't care.

"Rosin was using the passages to try to escape Rin and take Lineth with him," I said.

"Is she hurt?" Beran lurched to his feet.

"No, sir, but she's still in the passages and so are the Stonebridges. Not together," I added when I saw Beran's face.

Thien waved his hand. "Go on. Quickly."

I gabbled out my story of the well and what had happened there and who had been responsible, finishing with, "My friend Timur was killed trying to help."

"Brylla was trying to use the well to make herself younger?" Adrya asked, disbelief plain in her voice. I felt an odd relief. She hadn't been involved in this crime at all.

"I interfered," I said, "and now she's babbling and I think it's—"

"Enough talk." Beran strode toward the door. "I'm going to find Lineth. Open a passage for me, Jarka."

Thien put up a hand. "Wait. It sounds as if Lineth is safe and Rosin is trapped. We need to know what we're dealing with." He turned to Adrya. "You knew about these passages?"

"I did," Adrya said with far more dignity than I could have managed. "Castle Wysmen and Wyswomen have always known."

Beran shifted from foot to foot. I heard his breath coming in angry huffs.

"Who else knows?" Thien asked.

It dawned on me that Thien had moved past being surprised or angry and on to considering the advantage he might be able to draw from the passages. But what would he do to work justice?

Beran yanked the door open but hovered on the threshold.

"Jarka's the only one who knows," Adrya said. "Well, and evidently all the Stonebridges."

"Lineth knows now, of course," I said, "because Rosin took her there. And Ellyn, the girl who takes care of the kids in the refuge. She came with me to rescue my cousin.

A guard is in the refuge to protect the kids too. I had to tell him so he could guard the entrance there. Oh, and Laren."

Adrya groaned and dropped her head in her hands. "So many! Who's Laren?"

"A kid at the refuge. He's about three, I think."

"The Stonebridges will be in no position to speak," Thien said in a tone that sent ice sliding down my spine. Maybe justice would be worked after all. "And their fate should warn the others to silence. Except possibly the three-year-old. That's a tongue that's hard to stop, but people tend to dismiss what children say." He drummed his fingers on the table. "This may work out if we're careful. Adrya, you and Jarka go look for Lady Lineth."

"I'm going too," Beran said. As if anyone with eyes hadn't already seen that.

Again, Thien said, "Of course. Get a search going in the castle for the Stonebridges too in case they left the passages. If they're still in there, find them and lock them up somewhere they can't tell anyone. And," he added as Adrya rose, "when you've finished, come back here. I want to consult you on a matter concerning my son and Lady Lineth."

Beran vanished down the hall, with Adrya scrambling to keep up. I lingered. I'd never have another chance to do this. "Lady Lineth would make a wonderful queen."

Thien regarded me levelly.

I forced myself onward. "Folks in Rin love her too because of the way she's taking care of stray kids at the refuge. That may not mean much to the nobles who've come in from the country, but it means a lot to the folks in town."

"When I want your advice, I'll ask for it," Thien said.

I fought the urge to huddle in a safe corner. I was in a small room with a powerful man, but Thien wasn't Clovyan, and I was going to speak up. "A Wysman advises the king."

Thien's voice was stony. "I was unaware you were already a Wysman."

And since Adrya dismissed me, I never would be one. With no ready answer, I followed the others to start the search for Lineth.

THE ONLY SOUND from the round room was the musical ripple of falling water. I followed Adrya and Beran inside and stood looking down at where I'd last seen Brylla and Dugan. Adrya knew the passages well, and she'd led us straight here, though I didn't think she was happy to be in this room. The light from her lantern shimmied and her knuckles shone white on its handle. She drew a deep breath and turned to me so she no longer saw the glowing water. "Were Brylla and Dugan well enough to leave on their own?" she asked.

"Dugan was. He'd have to help his mother though, unless she was a whole lot saner than she was when I saw her."

"Are they a threat to Lineth?" Beran asked.

"Dugan could be if he left his mother. Brylla probably not. She was…" I groped for words to describe what Brylla was like. "She was seeing things."

"Like you do?" Beran asked.

"No." The word exploded from my mouth. "She sounded mad."

"I can't believe this place is here." Beran's voice was tight. "His Majesty should have been told. When this is over, it needs to be destroyed."

"Think twice, sir," Adrya said. Beran gave her a sharp look. "Wysones have left it in place because one or two of the old texts suggest that at the start, the well was meant to serve as a way to give good things to other people."

Beran bit out his words. "That was a long time ago. People have changed."

"Maybe," I said. "Or maybe it's just that magic is fading from the world, so it doesn't work well anymore." At that moment, I couldn't feel the castle's usual throb of elemental power at all.

"I don't care." Beran's mouth pressed in a thin line. "I want it gone." He looked back out into the dark passage. "Which way is Lineth?" he asked me.

I bit my lip. "I think just straight up that way, but every time I've been in here, I've got lost."

Beran strode off, his sword in his hand, as it had been since we entered the passages. Adrya and I hurried after him with our lanterns. We worked our way along the passage until it dead ended in a crossing. Adrya and Beran both looked at me.

I lifted my shoulders. "Left, I think."

"You think," Beran repeated.

"Please, lower your voices," Adrya whispered. "The king will be unhappy if we're heard. Moreover, Rosin could be just around the corner."

"Do the Powers love me that much?" Beran had dropped his voice, but I heard the quiver of anticipation.

Adrya must have heard it too. She caught Beran's arm and waited until the prince turned before she spoke. "I was at the Battle of Lac's Holding, sir," Adrya said. "We would be wise to prevent another such battle if we can."

Beran eyed Adrya's hand on his arm and said nothing.

Adrya let the prince go, and Beran jerked his head for me to begin searching again.

We rounded a corner. Another hall stretched away with the dark gap of a stairway looming on the left. My mind busy with a vision of a sword-wielding Rosin, I held my lantern toward the stairwell as Beran slipped forward sword extended.

A pale face stared out at us. An arm swung back. "No!" I ducked. Lineth had cocked her arm to whip her leather belt at anyone who came near. At her feet, Timur's body was draped up the steps. For an instant, Lineth froze. Then she flung the belt aside and launched herself into Beran's open arms.

He caught her to him, his sword tilted carefully away from her back. "Are you all right? Did that snake hurt you?"

"Shh," Adrya warned.

Lineth's voice was muffled against Beran's chest, but she sounded as if she might be crying. "I am fine, fine." Her hands left smears of filth on the back of Beran's jerkin.

"I'm so sorry I wasn't here," Beran said.

"I told your father—" Lineth began.

"I know," Beran said.

Lineth sniffled inelegantly and swiped the back of her hand under her nose. Beran fumbled at his pocket. When he came up empty of a handkerchief, he slid the end of his sleeve down over his hand and tenderly wiped Lineth's nose.

I stared down at Timur with grief swelling in my throat. He'd been only too right when he swore he'd never leave the castle.

Beran peered over the top of Lineth's head. "That's Timur?"

"Yes, sir." I looked up at him. "He came with me to keep me safe. I owe him."

"Then so do I," Beran said. "Believe me that's a debt the Stonebridges will pay."

A shiver ran down my spine. I didn't usually think of Beran as frightening, but right that moment, he was terrifying.

"You should take Lady Lineth and Timur's body out

of here, sir," Adrya said. "If you go up these stairs and straight ahead, there's a door. Do you remember how to use the runes? Give Lady Lineth your lantern, Jarka."

I offered Lineth the light. She pushed free of Beran's grip and took it.

Beran ran his gaze over me and Adrya and then looked down at Lineth. I could almost see his thoughts. He wanted Lineth out of there, but he doubted the prudence of abandoning a woman and a crippled boy with Rosin and maybe Dugan around.

Adrya must have seen the same thing. "We'll be safe enough. Dugan is unwell, and Rosin and I have known one another since childhood. He'd never hurt me."

The lantern in Lineth's hand swayed. Beran glanced at her, then extended his sword to Adrya. "Do you know how to use it?"

"No, sir," Adrya said. "You should keep it."

Beran flicked a look at me and sheathed the sword, which was smart. I'd never even held one. He cradled Timur's body in his arms. "I'll come back for Rosin. If he turns up, watch where he goes and wait for me."

"The next passage on the right is the one Rosin went down," Lineth said.

"We'll keep an eye out for him," Adrya said.

Lineth started up the stairs, holding the lantern aloft and glancing frequently over her shoulder at Beran. The light faded.

"You've known Rosin since childhood?" I said. "How

well?"

She sighed. "I admit I loved him once, but it was a girl's love, and in the end, I chose studying in Rin." Her mouth twisted. "It was perhaps the most Wys decision I've ever made." She slid the panel on her lantern nearly shut, so it cast only a dim glow, then handed it to me and strode toward the passage Lineth had named.

Still absorbing her admission, I scrambled after her. "Aren't we waiting for Beran?"

"I intend to deal with Rosin myself," she said.

"Like you did nine years ago?" I let my voice rise. "Did you advise Thien to let him go because you once loved him?"

"Perhaps," she said, "though that wasn't what I thought I was doing. And I did go to Stonebridge Manor and confiscate all his uncle's books. My mistake was that I couldn't bear to burn them. Hush now."

At the next crossway, she halted and looked in each of the three directions we could take. I raised the lantern. Overhead, something moved. I jumped before realizing all I'd seen were cobwebs swaying in the air drifting through the tunnel.

Adrya turned into the breeze. She drew a deep breath, and, as she let it out, she muttered something.

"What did you say?" I asked.

For a heartbeat, Adrya was silent. "Nothing. A word from the old tongue. This way." She led me down the passage. I'd lost all sense of how far we'd gone when Adrya murmured, "Wait." Ahead, light bobbed toward us from a hallway that dead-ended in the one we were in.

My heart quickened. "You're not going to let him go again, are you?" I whispered. I tried frantically to think of some way to stop that from happening.

She hushed me and pointed to a spot along the wall. "Wait there." She took the lantern from me and closed it completely. I barely heard the tap of it being set down and the shuffle of Adrya's feet moving away. Sweat plastered my shirt to my spine. The approaching light grew brighter, and firm footsteps drew near.

"Going somewhere, Rosin?" Adrya asked.

Rosin's lantern clanged to the floor and careened around, showing him leaping backward, waving his sword. He planted his feet and swiveled from me to Adrya. Dried blood edged a cut on his cheek. One of Ellyn's stones must have found its target. Gaze on Adrya, he dipped his sword slightly. "I have to say I'm glad to see you, Adrya," he said. "How about escorting me out of here?"

"No," I said.

"Jarka, I won't tell you again to hold your tongue," Adrya said sharply. Rosin lowered his sword further. "Rosin, you should know that Prince Beran has returned. At present, he is escorting Lady Lineth to safety. If you wish to be safe too, you will allow me to show you to a secure place before His Highness comes looking for you."

Rosin's smile broadened. "Excellent. Show me out, and I'll go home, and things will settle down the way they did before." His voice was warm. He reached a hand out to her. "You and I have been friends and more than friends for too long to wish one another harm."

Adrya shook her head. "You never change, do you? Come. I'll show you to safety."

I lunged to block Rosin's way along the passage. The point of his sword slid to within a hand's breadth of my chest. My heart threatened to kick its way out through my ribs, but I didn't move. Instead, I considered whether it would be possible to knock the sword away with my crutch. If I did, what would Adrya do? Would she help me or her old friend, Rosin?

"Move, Jarka." Behind Rosin, I saw Adrya take a step toward us. "Don't hurt him, Rosin." When he glanced over his shoulder, she said, "You can trust me."

I blinked. She was looking straight at me. Was she telling *me* to trust her? I no longer trusted even Lyssa. I had faith in Lineth and more or less in Beran. Despite how briefly I'd known her, I'd trust Ellyn with my life assuming I hadn't made her angry. But beyond them, the only person I trusted was me. Street kids learned that lesson the hard way. Timur had forgotten it, trusted me, and died.

"I act as always for the good of Rinland," Adrya said, "the way a Wysone should."

Rosin turned back to me. "You heard her, boy. Get out of our way."

I thought about the kids in the refuge being looked after at this very moment. Was their trust stupid? What kind of person had Adrya shown herself to be in the months I'd known her? Feeling as if I were crossing some huge, treacherous crack in the earth, I stepped aside.

Adrya gestured, and Rosin walked past me. I stayed well away from him and his sword. "Put that away, Rosin," Adrya said. "You're frightening him." She picked up a lantern.

Rosin snorted but sheathed his sword.

I hustled to Adrya's side, struggling to keep up as she set her usual brisk pace. At one corner, Rosin hesitated, but Adrya kept going. "We need to hurry if we don't want Beran here breathing fire," she said. She turned down a short corridor, slid through a narrow opening, and waited in front of a line of runes for us to catch up. "Open it, Jarka." She squeezed aside to let me and Rosin through. I heard a tap as she set the lantern on the floor.

I raised my hand, hesitated, and then swept it down and said the words. The door swung away from me. I stepped through to find myself at the back of a long hallway with a line of closed doors on either side and another closed door at the far end. In front of that door sat Thien's jailer, his eyes goggling at the sight of us. Adrya had guided us to the jail.

Someone stumbled into my back. I fell, tangled in my crutch and what turned out to be Rosin's flailing arms. Adrya stomped on him and yanked his sword free of its sheath. "Help us," she called to the jailer who was already on his feet, barreling toward us. By the time I'd dragged myself out from under Rosin, the jailer was hauling him up with his arms pinned behind him.

"Lock him up," Adrya panted. Her hair had come loose from its knot and straggled around her face.

"Bitch!" Rosin cried. "You lied to me!"

The jailer shoved him into a cell, slammed the door, and locked it with a key hanging from a nearby hook. He added the key to the ring on his belt.

Adrya stepped up to the barred window. "I promised to lead you to safety and I did. Be glad there are bars between you and Beran." She turned to the jailer. "Tell no one he's here. I'll hold you responsible if His Highness gets wind of his whereabouts." When the jailer's eyes widened in alarm, she added, "It won't be for long. He'll be needed at the fealty ceremony tomorrow." She hooked her hair behind her ears and beckoned me to follow her out of the jail.

As I passed the third cell on the left, Clovyan's face peered through the barred window. "Jarka, you stupid bastard. Look what you've done. You've abandoned the way decent people act with their family."

I skidded to a halt. "Not me, Clovyan. You." I felt a surge of satisfaction.

"Lyssa won't thank you," he snarled.

I started walking again, going toward where Adrya waited with the door ajar.

"Who do you think she'll choose?" Clovyan shouted. "You or me?"

The door closed on Clovyan still shouting insults. I tried to block what he said out of my head and heart. Lyssa had betrayed the kid I was when he beat me. He wasn't telling me anything new.

We started across the old keep. "You didn't tell Rosin about his wife and son being hurt," I said.

Her mouth tightened. "I didn't think he'd care."

I flinched. From the main courtyard, I could hear music and laughter. It felt like it came from a different world. Not simpler or more mysterious or easier or harder, but sure as spring, different. The question trembling on my tongue felt out of place in the sunshine. I asked it anyway. "How did you know which way to go to find Rosin?"

Instead of answering, she said, "That was your cousin's brute of a husband? He obviously can't be allowed to go back to her. As I recall, she's a seamstress. The castle could always use another good one." Inside my head, I was still running through what she said, when she quickened her pace. "Don't dawdle. I have to see His Majesty, and I need to do my hair first." She cut her eyes sideways at me. "You did well, Jarka."

I was out of breath trying to keep up. "Adrya? I want to find where they put my friend Timur and stand vigil."

I thought she might protest that I was wasting my time, but she simply said, "That's the right thing to do. Go."

I found him in the infirmary. When the healer pulled

back the sheet to show me his face, he looked like he was asleep—peaceful and unafraid and terribly young.

"Will they put him in the city cemetery?" I asked.

"Does he have family in the city?" the healer asked.

I thought about Timur's granny. "Just me," I said.

"Then no. There's a crypt under the Great Hall. Castle household is buried there."

I dragged my sleeve over my face. Timur would stay in the castle forever after all. I nudged a stool closer with my crutch and sat next to him, keeping him company and waiting for the dawn of one of the two days of the year when light and dark were in balance.

# Chapter 21

I HURRIED ALONG the dimly lit castle corridor, straightening my shirt as I went. The hallways were quiet. I'd seen dawn gray the light outside the infirmary windows right before the page turned up with the news that Adrya wanted me. I reached the library, shoved my hair out of my eyes, and went in. The splash of the courtyard fountain drifted through the open window. The room still lay in shadows except for the pool of lantern light on the table next to which Adrya stood. In Adrya's usual chair sat Thien.

I halted so suddenly, I almost stumbled. I bowed to Thien and glanced at Adrya, but her face was unreadable. She'd reported to him without me. We must have come to the moment when I'd learn whether he'd work justice or not. In a way, it didn't matter. I was no longer part of Thien's service. Beran might keep me, but he might decide not to cross his father's Wyswoman. I didn't know what I was going to do now, but I no longer had to worry about what it meant to serve the powerful. Lyssa and Izzy would be safe here and I'd find work. I gripped my crutch. Surely I could find something. I wouldn't go back to living in the streets, would I?

Thien folded his hands on the table. "I sent for you, Jarka, because I thought you had a right to know what Adrya and I will keep as secret as we can from everyone else."

"Yes, sir." I tried to keep all judgment out of my voice.

"A short while ago," Thien said, "the tower guards found Brylla and Dugan hiding in a shed near the South Gate. He is still ill, and she is quite mad, spouting all sorts of nonsense and shrieking about visions."

"What will happen to them?" For reasons I didn't fully understand, I was uncertain what answer I wanted. Years ago, Thien had executed Rosin's uncle, and though Rena was still alive, Brylla and Dugan had committed the same crime. Still the thought of their deaths horrified me. This was one hard decision I was glad to have no part of.

"The Powers have already punished Brylla," Thien said. "I wouldn't dare to change what they've decreed. I'll send her to live in a guarded house on the western border. Dugan will go home with a guardian of my choosing. I intend to try to make a loyal lord out of him."

I thought it might be too late for that, but I kept my mouth shut. "And Lord Rosin, sir?"

Standing at Thien's side, Adrya shifted her weight.

"Since he had nothing to do with misusing the well, he'll keep his life but go with his wife," Thien said. "If he's wise, he'll be glad there are guards between him and my son."

I waited for a flush of vengeful anger. Instead, I felt only weary. "And me, sir?"

Thien raised an eyebrow. "What about you?"

"You are, of course, my apprentice," Adrya said.

That was news to me. I blinked at the king and then at Adrya. A small hope wriggled into my mind. Maybe I just wouldn't tell them about the suspicion that had grown on me in the passages. I dismissed the thought at once. They had a right to know. "Brylla's madness? Her visions? I think maybe I gave those to her in the Well of Sharing."

Thien tapped his signet ring against the table. "You are many things, Jarka, but you are not mad."

"That's not what I meant, sir. In the passages today, I felt different. And a wisp of wind down there ignored me. I felt nothing from it. I think maybe I gave Brylla the Powers' gift I use to read the wind. I'm not sure I can do it anymore."

Thien shrugged. "I can't see how that matters."

I clutched the edge of the table to upright.

"You're shrewd," Thien said, "and the way you've lived has made you wary and good at sensing trouble. If Beran decides he needs a wind reader, he can find one, but if he asks me, I'll tell him that even if he does, he should keep you too." Thien rose. "It will be interesting to see how the fealty ceremony goes. Eh, Adrya?" With a feral smile, the king left the room.

I sank onto a stool, trying to convince myself I wasn't back in the dormitory dreaming. I was apparently not done with living in the castle yet, not done with advising the powerful.

Adrya seated herself where the king had been. "Are you all right?"

I smiled slowly. "I'm not sure." I thought of something. "What's the king going to do about Lineth and Beran?"

"He's still deciding. Thien always wants to be sure he's doing the right thing for Rinland. I did give him a bit of advice." One corner of Adrya's mouth lifted.

I raised an eyebrow.

"I told him Lineth had faced troubles with courage and become a stronger, more compassionate woman who understands the needs of her people. Indeed, the Powers might almost have sent her as a gift to Rinland. It's possible *The Book of the Wys* will tell us that at prayers this morning."

I whistled. "And I thought you had no guts."

Adrya smiled faintly. "You can't be a Wysone without guts."

"You don't challenge Thien openly though."

"Challenging a king openly isn't always the wisest option."

"I suppose not." I lowered my gaze to watch Adrya's

hands caressing the book that lay before her. One of the old ones, I realized. "What are you reading?"

Adrya frowned down at the pages. "I've been thinking about Rena and how she might be cured."

"Me too." For all the good it had done. I could only be grateful I'd found Izzy before she'd been harmed.

"I remembered this book." Adrya stroked the page. "It talks about people who drift between life and death and how something or someone needs to tip the balance and call them back."

I sat upright, my own worries forgotten. "How?"

"As usual, the Wysones weren't clear." Adrya ran a finger along a line of runes and read. "'Call them to you with the strength of the divine Powers, moving through their creation.'" She pursed her lips. "Perhaps that means prayer."

"Or channeling an element," I said.

Adrya grimaced.

"I saw you sensing what the wind had to say in those passages, Adrya. That's how you knew which way Rosin had gone, isn't it?" I reached out, hesitated, then laid my hand on the book next to Adrya's and waited. The parchment was smooth under my fingertips, but I felt nothing else, no throb of life. For a moment, grief choked me. I met Adrya's gaze. "You feel it, don't you?" Adrya pulled her hand into her lap and looked away. "It's a gift, Adrya, and maybe you can use it to help Rena." I leaned forward. "You're a Wyswoman. This is what you do, assuming you really do have guts."

Adrya looked back at the book. I counted to eight before she rose. "We might as well try."

I jumped to my feet and rushed to open the door. I had to hold myself back to stay at Adrya's side through the dawn-quiet corridors and across the courtyard. The street outside the gate was deserted. I led the way to the refuge and mounted the front step while Adrya ran her gaze over the castle wall looming over us. "They should have been safe here." She frowned.

I knocked on the door and we waited. Somewhere down in the city, a rooster crowed. Another echoed him. I knocked again. Someone tugged at the latch from inside. A childish voice called, "Wait." A moment later, the door opened a crack, and Ellyn peeked through. She was dressed in something white—her nightgown, I realized, and raised my eyes hastily to her face. It was the first time we'd seen one another since we brought Izzy out of the passages.

"Are you all right?" I asked.

"Yes. And you? The guard we left here came back with word from the king, but all he said was I was to hold my tongue about what happened."

"I'm unhurt, and I got the same orders."

Behind her, a kid's voice asked who had come. Ellyn looked back into the room. "Every one of you, get back in bed. It's too early to get up."

"I think the Darklight treats already came," the kid

said.

"In bed! Right now!"

"Who is it, Ellyn?" That was Tally's voice.

"Jarka and Wyswoman Adrya."

Adrya stepped us beside me. "We've come to see if we can help Rena."

Ellyn's eyes widened. She opened the door, and Adrya and I went into the refuge. The kids were all in bed, but I could see the blankets wriggling. The shutters were closed, and a single lamp burned on a table near the door. Whatever was on the table was hidden by a long cloth. The room smelled faintly of cinnamon.

"I'll stay out here and keep an eye on them." Tally swept a narrow-eyed look along the line of cots and movements ceased.

Ellyn led us to the back room, where the covers were thrown aside on her bed and Tally's, and Rena and Laren lay in their cots. The space was already so crammed that Adrya and I could barely press in with her. When my arm bumped hers, she shuffled aside, clutching the neck of her nightgown closed. She smelled of warm skin and sleep.

Laren sat up, knuckling his eyes and frowning from me to Adrya. "Go away," he said.

"Would you like me to go?" Ellyn asked. "I could take Laren."

"No." Laren stuck out his lower lip. "Gonna stay with Rena. Gonna sleep in her bed." He slid off his own cot, eeled between me and Adrya, and clambered up next to

Rena.

"You have to come with me or sleep in your own bed." As Ellyn bent to pick him up, her nightgown gaped. I tried not to look, but my foot was the only broken part of me. The rest worked fine.

"I think you should stay, Ellyn," Adrya said. "Indeed, I believe Laren should stay with his sister."

Looking pleased with himself, Laren nestled down next to Rena and flung his arm over her.

"Ellyn, you take one of Rena's hands," Adrya said. "Jarka, you take the other."

I obeyed. Rena's hand lay limp in mine. Her braids fell away from an empty face.

Adrya's eyes flicked over the scene in front of her. Now that she'd decided to try what she could do, she was as determined as I'd ever seen her. She extended her hands over Rena, drew a deep breath, and closed her eyes. Silence filled the room except for faint whispering and stirring from the kids pretending to sleep in the big room.

"Divine Powers," Adrya said, "selfish people have misused your gifts and harmed this child who should have been protected by our watchful care. We ask your help in calling her back to us despite our failure."

I flinched. I'd certainly failed in looking out for Rena. I'd all but put her right into Dugan's hands. Lines creased the spot between Ellyn's brows as she looked at Rena. I thought I could see what her face would look like when she was forty, and decided it would be beautiful because it would show the depth of her care. She must feel guilty too, I realized, though that was silly. She'd done the best she could.

"Rena," Adrya said, "we beg you to come again to Laren, who loves you, and Ellyn, who cares for you. Come back to Jarka, who champions the helpless as the Powers would have us all do."

I held my breath and waited.

Adrya's hands trembled, then shook. She threw her head back and arched her spine. Her teeth clattered. Beneath my touch, Rena stirred and opened her eyes.

"Rena! Rena!" Laren cried.

She yanked her hands free, rolled toward him, and hugged him.

Adrya staggered, then leaned limply against the foot of Rena's cot, her face glistening with sweat. She stared at Rena and Laren, mouth open, astonished.

My hand falling to my side, I watched Rena and Laren. The Powers had acted here. Power had flowed, and I'd felt nothing. It was a selfish thought, but I couldn't help it.

"Well," Adrya huffed.

"It takes some getting used to," I said.

Ellyn dropped to her knees next to Rena's bed. When she looked up at Adrya, tears were running down her face. "Thank you seems too weak a thing to say for giving a child her life back."

I remembered how Ellyn had talked about the death of her little brother and thought maybe Adrya had given

Ellyn a bit of her life back too. I was glad, but I wished I'd been the one to do it.

"Jarka, we should be going," Adrya said. "These children need to sleep."

Ellyn rose. "Wyswoman, may I speak to Jarka for a moment?"

"Of course." Adrya paused in the room's doorway.

Ellyn waited, face going pink.

"Oh." Adrya pulled herself erect. "Yes. I'll see you at prayers, Jarka." She walked along the line of cots, past an astonished looking Tally, and slipped out into the dawn.

Ellyn pushed the small room's door most of the way shut. She glanced at Rena and Laren, lying in one another's arms but watching us from under drooping lids. "Go to sleep," she said. "Close your eyes."

"Yes, Miss Ellyn." Laren pressed as close to Rena's side as he could get and squeezed his eyes shut. Rena's gaze was fuzzy. Her lids drifted down.

Ellyn turned to me. "I know you can't say what happened in the passages, but is something the matter?"

I decided I must be as transparent as the kids fidgeting in their cots. "Not really. I'd be ungrateful to say that."

"But?" she said.

I drew a deep breath. She deserved to know the truth. "I've lost my feel for the way the Powers move in the elements. The king and Adrya aren't disturbed, but Beran wanted me because I was a wind reader. If he still wants that, I might never become a Wysman."

"Don't be a fool."

I blinked.

"Wind reading didn't save Izzy," Ellyn said. "Courage and love did. *Your* courage and love."

"They wouldn't have been enough," I said. "The Powers helped me."

"The Powers wouldn't have been enough on their own either," Ellyn said. "Besides, you saved Lady Lineth. If Beran sends you away now, I'll wear my gown inside out for a month. And anyway, what makes you think I'd care if you became something other than a Wysman?" She was breathing hard and leaning toward me, face fierce.

I put up my hands, palms out. "Yes, Miss Ellyn."

She grabbed a paper-wrapped package from the writing table and whacked me with it. Fortunately it turned out to be soft. "I meant to do this gracefully, but you're provoking sometimes, Jarka. This is for you." She thrust the package into my hands. "A Darklight gift."

I turned it over, feeling a smile grow. No one had given me a Darklight gift since I was ten.

"You should wait until tomorrow to open it," Ellyn said.

I yanked at the string tying the package shut, and the paper fell away. A blue wool scarf unfolded to its full length, one end in my hands, the other nearly brushing the floor. I recognized it. I'd seen it often enough on the rocking chair in the refuge, growing longer each day.

"When I started it, I didn't know who it was for," Ellyn

said, "and I know spring is here, but it's still chilly. I thought you might need it."

"It's beautiful." I draped it over one arm and drew out the object I'd been carrying tucked in my belt. "I found it in the well room. I'm not sure this counts as a gift," I said anxiously, "but it's yours and you should have it."

"My knife!" She seized it, eyes widening. Then she stretched and kissed my cheek. My ears got hot. "Thank you. And thank you for asking the castle to send all those Darklight treats." She nodded towards the table by the door.

"I didn't," I said.

She drew in her chin. "A kitchen helper came with the cakes just after the kids were all asleep. He said a boy told them the king had ordered it."

"A boy? Like a page?"

"I asked if it was you, and he said he didn't know, but I just assumed."

"I'm glad you have them. I wish I'd thought of it." We stood in silence. I became aware that I was with a girl in her nightgown in her bedroom. "I should go," I said.

She took my hand and led me out into the large room. With a faint smile, Tally went back into the small room. At the door, I stopped, trying to think of something to say so I could stay a little longer.

Ellyn frowned past me, gaze on the table of treats. "How did they do that with Tally right here?" she asked, exasperation in her voice.

I turned to see what she was looking at. One corner of the cloth had been folded back and a plate was empty except for a few crumbs of what looked like Darklight cake. I thought of what she'd said. An unknown boy ordered the treats. I swallowed and darted a look around the room.

"What?" she said.

"Nothing," I said. But my heart lifted. I thought, I hoped, a ghost had taken up residence in the refuge he'd needed. A ghost who gobbled cakes.

I let go of Ellyn's hand and went out into the pink and gold new day.

LIMBS RIGID, FACE pale, Rosin walked the length of the Great Hall and dropped to one knee in front of Thien. His voice shook as he recited the fealty oath the lords had been taking all morning. The crowd in the Hall hushed. As far as I knew, no one had been told about the passages or anything that happened in them, but everyone had heard that Dugan was ill and Brylla had gone mad. Bizarrely enough rumors that the Grabber had struck were flying from mouth to mouth. I suspected Adrya had set them working and, when I thought about it, there was a shred of truth in the old tale. Over the years, bad things must have happened at the Well of Sharing. Legend had explained them by supplying an evil figure to carry them out.

I leaned farther around the doorway from the waiting room to the Hall, so I could see Beran standing behind Thien with Lineth at his side. Beran regarded Rosin from under half-lowered lids, reminding me unexpectedly of his father. Lineth didn't even seem to notice Rosin's presence. Instead, she looked at Beran. The gossip about Rosin's family was likely to be lost in a much more exciting story. The king had made up his mind and today would include a celebration of their existing marriage as well as the feast of Darklight.

I wrapped Ellyn's scarf around my neck. I had something I wanted to do while everyone else was busy. I made my way through the courtyards and up to the castle walkway where I set up the wind box Lineth had handed over when I knocked on her door just before prayers. We'd both ignored the dusty man's shirt hanging on a chair back behind her. I flung the colored paper and blew on it. With one part of my head, I knew this was pointless, but I'd lived with the surge of elemental power so long that I had to be sure. The paper settled into bright heaps. I waited, but I felt only the way the cold was making my nose run, heard only the voices and footsteps of the folks already emerging into the main courtyard, eager for the start of the Darklight Day celebrations. For a moment, my throat swelled with loss. *That feeling was never yours anyway*, I reminded myself. *You only leaned on the strength of the Powers.*

Across the river, the sun coaxed the new crops higher.

Thien's minstrel struck up a lively tune in the courtyard. I scooped paper bits into their pouch, collapsed the box, and shoved them both into my bag. It was best to move on. When you got stuck in the past, you were just stuck, like Rosin longing for youth or Brylla destroying herself and maybe her son to hang onto her husband.

I knotted the blue scarf more securely around my neck and started down the stairs to the old keep courtyard.

"There you are."

I halted as the steward bustled up. "Did you want me?"

The steward rubbed his hand through his hair leaving bits of it on end. As the holiday had worn on, he'd grown more and more harried looking. "Prince Beran told me to consult with you about something. You know he always sends coins to be handed out at New Square as his Darklight gift to the people."

I nodded. I'd collected a few of those coins myself, when I could elbow my way through the crowd on my crutch to get to them.

"His Highness is concerned that the ill and the old are too infirm to get to New Square and benefit from his gift," the steward said. "He told me to ask you if you have any ideas how that might be done better."

"You mean for today? That's short notice!"

The steward made an apologetic face. "I know, but he's been gone. Anything you can come up with by this afternoon would be welcome."

"I'll think on it."

The steward trotted away, and I followed more slowly, realizing that I felt a bit better. Today was today, and I'd see what it brought me. I was no longer Jarka who could read the wind, but I was someone still. I just had to figure out who. Someone shrewd and wary, as Thien said, but also someone who could care about a girl and have her care about him back, and someone who could help a prince help the poor. Maybe that was power enough.

# Dear Reader

Thank you for reading *The Wysman*. If you enjoyed this book (or even if you didn't) please visit the site where you purchased it and write a brief review. Your feedback is important to both me and my publisher, and it will help other readers decide whether to read the book, too.

# About the Author

At one time, Winsor taught technical writing at Iowa State University and GMI Engineering & Management Institute (now Kettering). She then discovered that writing fiction is much more fun and has never looked back. If you visit Winsor's blog and sign up for her newsletter, she'll send you a free short story.

Dorothy A. Winsor writes young adult and middle grade fantasy. Her novels include Finders Keepers (Zharmae, 2015), Deep as a Tomb (Loose Leave Publishing, 2016), and The Wind Reader (Inspired Quill, 2018).

Find the author via her website:

www.dawinsor.com

Or tweet at her: @dorothywinsor

# More From This Author

## The Wind Reader

Stuck in a city far from home, street kid Doniver fakes telling fortunes so he can earn a few coins to feed himself and his friends. Then the divine Powers smile on him when he accidentally delivers a true prediction for the prince.

Concerned about rumors of treason, the prince demands that Doniver use his "magic" to prevent harm from coming to the king, and so Doniver is taken— dragged?—into the castle to be the royal fortune teller.

Now Doniver must decide where the boundaries of honor lie, as he struggles to work convincing magic, fend off whoever is trying to shut him up, and stop an assassin, assuming he can even figure out who the would-be assassin *is*. All he wants is to survive long enough to go home to the Uplands, but it's starting to look as if that might be too much to ask.

Paperback ISBN: 978-1-908600-75-2
eBook ISBN: 978-1-908600-76-9

Available from all major online and offline outlets.